BLACK WIDOW

A GIA SANTELLA CRIME THRILLER
BOOK 4

KRISTI BELCAMINO

LIQUID MIND PUBLISHING

Liquid Mind Publishing
This is a work of fiction. All characters, names, places and events are the product of the author's imagination or used fictitiously.

GIA SANTELLA CRIME THRILLER SERIES

Enjoying the Gia Santella series? Scan below to order more books today!

Vendetta

Vigilante

Vengeance

Black Widow

Day of the Dead

Border Line

Night Fall

Stone Cold

Cold as Death

Cold Blooded

Dark Shadows

Dark Vengeance

Dark Justice

Deadly Justice

Deadly Lies

PROLOGUE

Somewhere off the coast of Africa

Silver moonlight sparkled on the waves below.

I leaned over the rail as the luxury cruise ship cut silently through the smooth Mediterranean Sea headed toward yet another port.

Italy was out there somewhere across the vast dark waters, invisibly tugging at my soul, triggering memories of another summer night gazing on this same moon from the balcony of an Italian villa.

It was on that night—with despair engulfing me and grief clawing at my insides—that I realized my inescapable destiny: to always be alone.

The man I loved had just been murdered at a wedding reception, proof positive that everyone I cared for ended up dead.

Now, I stood on the Riviera Deck in the spaghetti-strapped, ankle-length, white beaded dress I'd worn to the formal dinner earlier and welcomed the chill that ran across my back, neck and arms. I let the wind whip my hair around my face so it would hide the traitorous tears streaming down cheeks.

Even though I was alone on the deck—everyone else long since in bed—I was embarrassed to be seen weeping, to be caught feeling sorry for myself.

I had more than most people could wish for in a lifetime. Except someone to love.

At least I'd made a new friend on this trip.

Natasha was one of the first women I'd ever met who seemed to meet me on equal ground. She wasn't cattily eyeballing me and making snide comments like many of the women I'd met on this cruise—well, hell, in my life.

Instead, when we first met, she snaked her arm through mine and said, "I think you're my type of woman, Giada Valentina Santella."

For the past week, we'd been buddies. We'd had tapas in Cartagena, smoked weed together at an Ibiza villa, soaked in ancient Arab baths, and hung out with the Barbary apes and dolphins in Gibraltar.

Having a female friend was something brand new to me. On most days, we started out meeting at the pool. I had to admit I looked forward to seeing Natasha walk up in her black one-piece swimsuit, tossing her long red hair and flashing her brilliant smile. When she walked up, every man in the vicinity stopped and stared.

Her husband, Henry, was much older and his doctor had advised him not to take the shore excursions, so Natasha and I were on our own.

It had been a good time.

Until tonight. Henry and Natasha had argued at dinner and then dismissed me. It'd hurt my feelings, but let's face it, I was the third wheel on their romantic cruise.

I'd been lucky to tag along for as long as I had. Normally Henry went to bed early, and we'd either hit the dance club—until they kicked us out; drink in the Star Bar—until they kicked us out, or grab our own bottles and sit on the Sun Deck by the pool with blankets pulled over us and talking and drinking and smoking until dawn.

For the most part, Natasha had treated her husband like a doting granddaughter would—kissing him on the cheek and treating him in a solicitous manner. But now something was off. As soon as dessert was served, Natasha had whispered something to Henry at dinner and his face had grown dark. He'd hissed something back and Natasha's eyes had grown wide. Then, they both stood and left.

For a split second, I'd wondered if it'd been something I did. But then thought, fuck that shit and ordered a few more drinks.

Finally, when the staff had cleaned up and I was the only one left, a kindly man in a white waiter suit approached and kicked me out of the dining room. I'd grown comfy slumped in my blue velvet, upholstered chair, tipping them back.

I headed for the Star Bar on the Baja Deck and, feeling fancy, ordered a cognac.

My attempts to have a friend had left me lonelier than ever. Maybe my only friend was the bottle. Now, that's a healthy attitude. I ignored the group of men at the other end of the bar, talking and staring at me.

After a long while, it was just me and Sal, the bartender. It wasn't his real name, but since he looked a little like my attorney back in California, I just started calling him that. He didn't seem to object since I was paying for each drink with an Andrew Jackson and telling him to keep the change. I think he would've kept serving me until Christmas, but some uptight fuck in a suit eventually came over and whispered to him at the same time all the lights came on.

"Why don't you go to bed now?" The dude in the suit said. I squinted my eyes at him and scowled.

Fuck that.

The last thing I wanted to do was go back to my lonely suite and sleep.

I'd sleep when I was dead.

The truth was, lying alone in the dark always brought back memories of Bobby, and I wouldn't be able to keep them at bay while I was three sheets to the wind. When sober, I could distract myself from the flood of painful memories. But shitfaced? Forget about it.

When it became clear the suit wouldn't leave without me, I slipped off my stool. "I'll go as soon as you do."

I knew I was being rude, but I stared him down until he left, giving me one last nasty look as he stepped through a door into the back. Sal, the sweetheart and adorable enabler, slipped me a half-full bottle of bourbon and winked at me. I shoved the bottle in my bag and headed for the Sun Deck.

I plopped on a cushy lounge chair and pulled a blanket up to my neck, lying back and taking in the stars. They were mesmerizing at sea. My eyelids grew heavy.

When I woke, the stars were gone, and the sky seemed a tiny bit lighter. A huge full moon hung low on the horizon. I still wanted to avoid the specter of my empty bed and suite, so I took the short flight of stairs to the Riviera Deck. I stood at the rail searching the dark sea in front of me. For what I didn't know.

For a second, I wondered how it would feel to just let myself tip over the rail, freefall into the swirling blue water below. But then I pulled back. I was a survivor. I was just having a bad night. It was normal. Bobby had been murdered not so far from here in the small Italian city of Positano. No wonder I was feeling shitty. It was difficult to be on the Mediterranean when not that long ago, I'd looked out on this same sea with the man I loved.

Checking out wasn't an option. Because if I had nothing else going for me, I had this: I wasn't a quitter.

I took a slug from my bourbon bottle, brushed my hair back behind my ears and squared my shoulders. The silvery moon was so fucking brilliant hanging low in the black velvet sky that I couldn't help but feel a sliver of hope. Any world that had something that goddamn beautiful was worth living in.

That's when I heard the scream—a long, piercing cry that split the pre-dawn silence like a sharp dagger.

1

TWO-BIT JUNKIE CRACK WHORE

B efore
     San Francisco

"THAT BITCH!"

My voice startled Django, who jumped, making the tags on his collar jangle. He'd been snoozing on his massive suede cushion near my bed.

"Sorry," I said to my dog and clicked off the show with my remote. "But she's a total pain. Who does she think she is?"

The previous few weeks, I'd become obsessed with rich, real housewives and their atrocious behavior.

It kept my mind off my own life.

Django stood and did his elaborate series of stretches. Paws and legs extended out front and then bent head to touch them.

Dust swirled in a beam of sunlight stretching across the length of the loft. I tried to remember the last time I'd swept. Then shrugged. No idea. Weeks. Maybe months.

The kitchen was the only part of my loft that was halfway clean and only because I hadn't cooked for weeks. Once a day I ate a delivered meal, usually Phở or chicken coconut soup and then bundled up my trash in a bag and sent it down the trash chute.

All my assorted belongings were scattered across my open loft space. Good thing I didn't own much. Mostly clothes and books and a few plants, with leaves that were now tipped brown. A pile of wilted, dirty clothes took up a decent chunk of real estate on the floor under my stainless-steel rolling clothes rack.

I hadn't run out of stuff to wear yet, but now the empty hangers on the rack outnumbered the full ones. I'd taken to wearing my leather pants any time I had to venture outside my home, which was once a week to my father's company. If I scraped my hair back in a tight ponytail, threw on red lipstick, high-heeled boots, and a blazer, I could almost pass for human.

That didn't mean the board members were fooled. I caught them giving me the side-eye and whispering under their breaths when they thought I wasn't paying attention.

"Shit!" I sat up, startling Django again. Poor thing wasn't used to me moving or talking.

Today was the day I was supposed to listen to the board's proposal from a Silicon Valley venture capitalist who had been wooing them for months. It was odd since most courting was usually done by the business owner, but after a national magazine had run an article on my combined live-work space developments for the homeless, we'd had investors knocking on our doors. It wasn't a bad spot to be in. We didn't need the investors—not really —but I sure as hell wasn't going to turn down someone shoving money my way.

I grabbed my watch.

"Fuck me!"

I'd completely missed the meeting. I unearthed my phone from my rumpled bed covers. Six missed calls. Four from the office. Two from Dante.

Damn it.

I missed my one chance to see him this week. I needed a dose of

Dante. Seeing my best friend was the one thing that got me out of bed lately.

Ever since I'd talked Dante out of his funk and brought him back home from Mexico, I'd fallen into my own dark hole. I couldn't seem to shake it. Although it should have helped me feel less lonely, having my best friend back in California seemed only to emphasize just how alone I was in this world. Dante was back, but he'd brought his new boyfriend, Silas.

He lived in Calistoga, north of San Francisco. He owned a trendy, five-star restaurant there and was opening a second location nearby. He was the main reason I got out of bed to attend the board meetings at my father's business. I had asked him to be my personal and professional adviser when I inherited the business.

I knew it was a pain in the ass for him to come down to San Francisco for our weekly meetings with the board, which made me feel even guiltier for missing the meeting today. I sucked.

I punched my pillow. Django side-eyed me and used his paw to hit the lever that opened the door to the roof. Even the dog knew better than to stick around when I was in a bad mood. His nails clicked on the stairs as he headed up to the rooftop garden to do his business. I was afraid to see how many turds were baking in the sun up there. I hadn't done poop patrol for at least two weeks.

I crawled back under the covers and closed my eyes. I'd sleep more and then see what the real housewives were up to. Something infuriating for sure.

I woke to the sound of Django yipping with happiness. Must be Thanh-Thanh. My neighbor downstairs walked Django for me twice a day. When she refused to take money for it, I lopped it off her rent. When she argued, I told her to deal with it or I wouldn't let her see Django anymore.

I was full of shit, but she bought it. Enough to pay less rent.

It used to be that my dog was all she cared about, but the other day a man had stood in the doorway behind her when she came to get Django. A beau! Damn skippy if she didn't deserve a man who made her smile and blush like he did.

I sat up in bed. "Thanh-Thanh?"

She poked her head in the door. She was holding the leash, and Django was twisting and twirling with excitement around her legs.

"How's your new man?"

Her cheeks grew red, and a smile I'd never seen before appeared on her face.

"That good, huh?"

"He's moving in." She blushed as she said it.

"Holy shit. Really?" But then I frowned. "Should I run a check on him. You know, have Darling check him out. Make sure he's good enough for you?"

"Oh, Gia. He's fine. I met his mom."

"Okay." That was always a good sign. "And he's good to her?"

"Very."

"Okay. Then. But I'm right up here if he doesn't treat you like a fucking princess, got it?"

"Oh, Gia." She blew out a big puff of air on her way out the door.

I flipped through the different TV channels looking for something to keep me busy until the next housewives show but could only find a Steve McQueen movie. It'd have to do.

I'd fallen asleep again when Django lost his mind barking again. Someone else was here.

Boy, was it busy around here today. I made a note to get all my keys back from my friends.

"Gia, Gia, Gia." Uh-oh. Darling. Her booming voice was near my head. I was afraid to peek out from my covers.

Darling was a bad ass. She had to be. She owned the largest hair salon in the San Francisco Tenderloin neighborhood, but she paid for her three massive homes with income from her side-gig providing anyone anywhere with a new identity and the paperwork to go with it. Darling had standards, though. She only provided false documents for people who were trying to escape impossible and dangerous situations.

I pulled the covers down from my face.

Her big Cleopatra eyes were wide, and she shook her head and made a "tsking" sound.

"You look like a two-bit junkie crack whore."

"Thanks, Darling. Love you too."

"Somebody gotta say it."

"I'm fine. Leave me alone." I covered my head again. But I was poised, listening for her reaction.

Darling gave an exaggerated sigh.

I held my breath as her footsteps moved toward the door. Oh my God, was she giving up so easily?

The door closed. I threw back my covers to see if she had tricked me and was still there. My loft was empty.

Fine. I didn't need her. Besides, why did she care all of a sudden? The past year she'd been so busy acting like a lovesick newlywed with her husband, George, she hadn't had any time for me.

I had to face it. Everybody was busy. Everybody had somebody special to love except me.

Dante had Silas. Darling had George. Thanh-Thanh had whatever-his-name-was-again.

Me? I had jack shit.

Everybody I ever loved had died.

My mother. My father. Bobby.

It was better that I stay alone. Safer for everybody that way. I couldn't deal with losing anyone else ever again.

My phone rang. I squinted to see who was calling.

Darling.

"Who are your female friends?" she said before I could even say hello.

"What?" Who cares?

"Who are your homegirls?"

I sat up. "You."

"I don't count. I'm old enough to be your mama. I mean your homegirls—the ones you go out with and talk on the phone with all the time."

Was she trying to make me feel like shit? If so, she was doing a damn good job.

"You're my friend," I said.

Exasperated sigh. "Fine. Who else?"

"Thanh-Thanh?"

"No. She's your nice neighbor. You guys have never once hung out or even had a conversation, have you?"

"No, but we could." If she weren't so gaga about her new boyfriend.

"Who are your homegirls, woman?"

"Nobody."

Checkmate. Mission accomplished, Darling. It's now official—I'm a total loser.

She brightened. "See, that's your problem. I don't know what I'd do without my homegirls. They listen to all my bitching about George."

"George is perfect."

She scoffed.

"Well, he is," I said. "Besides, I have Dante."

She ignored me. "My homegirls make me laugh. Make me cry. We share everything. That's what you need. Women like you. Your age. Your peers. Women you can confide in. Share personal stuff with."

I cringed. "I've never had a female friend like that."

"*What?*"

Even though she couldn't see me, I shrugged. I was damaged. Big shocker.

2

FLOATING DEATH TRAP

The next day I was still in bed when my door burst open, startling me out of a deep sleep.

"Oh, for fuck's sake!" I sat up, bleary-eyed, and fumbled for the Ruger 9mm under my pillow.

I held it out and then let my arm dangle and drop to the bed covers.

It was Darling.

And Dante. My best friend. In the flesh. In my loft.

Django, who just got a big fat F as a watch dog, hadn't even barked or made a peep when they'd come inside this time. Instead, he was at their feet, wiggling so much he was practically a blur.

"What's going on?" I asked.

"Intervention."

"An intervention is for addicts," I stretched. "I haven't even had a drink for ages."

"Well, that shows you need help," Dante said. His smile, a flash of white against his olive skin, was infectious.

"Stop," I said and kicked my legs over the side of the bed.

Darling bustled about in my galley kitchen, humming and

grinding coffee beans. "Intervention to save your friends from your smelly ass," she said.

"Not smelly." I sniffed my armpits and tried not to make a face.

She lifted a well-groomed eyebrow.

Okay. I probably smelled like death.

I watched it all from my perch in bed, blinking, speechless.

Meanwhile, Dante was leaning over my Bose speaker system.

Soon some Latin dance music was blaring throughout my loft. Dante swiveled his hips in the way only a sexy man could and started heading my way. He stuck out a finger, gesturing for me to get up and join him dancing.

I shook my head.

Despite myself, tears pricked the corners of my eyes. What was wrong with me? Seeing my friends made me ugly cry now?

Once my moka pot was percolating on the stove, Darling assembled a small breakfast feast on my kitchen table, pulling items from a bag: croissants and beignets.

Finally, Dante, gave up on getting me to dance. He turned down the music and plopped onto the bed beside me.

I couldn't stop grinning as I searched his face. "Why are you here? Really?"

"You flaked on us."

"I'm sorry. I slept in."

"You didn't even call."

True.

"And you didn't return my calls."

I didn't want to admit I hadn't even listened to his messages.

"I had to call Darling to see if you were even still alive."

"You know where I live." I said, defiantly crossing my arms across my chest.

"I barely made it to the board meeting. I had to rush back up to Calistoga. My new restaurant opens next week. It's crazy time."

"And yet, here you are." I grinned.

He exhaled and shook his head. "How many times do I have to rescue your ass?"

Taking my hand, he stood and pulled me to my feet. "Come eat."

"I'm not hungry."

"Look at you," he gestured at me. My clothes hung on me. "You're not looking good."

"Gee, thanks."

But I followed him to the table.

I was pretty sure a wave of funk accompanied me on the breeze as I walked to my kitchen table. Sitting on the far side of the table to spare them any smells, I broke off a small bite of the croissant and nibbled it. I gulped down some coffee, gratefully. I'd been having coffee delivered by the local market. I'd dubbed it bathwater coffee. But I drank it, knowing if I went cold turkey on my morning caffeine, I'd regret it.

I broke off another bite of croissant. Soon, before I had realized it, the entire thing was gone. I felt bloated and sick. It was the most I'd eaten in one sitting in some time.

When we were done, Dante opened the door to the roof.

"Let's go get some air."

Django raced ahead of the three of us.

I pulled a sweater on over my T-shirt and pajama pants. I grabbed a few plastic dog poop bags and followed him up the stairs.

My private rooftop garden sanctuary was looking sad. The plants were brown. Leaves had fallen onto the patio under my grapevine-strewn pergola. Small piles of dried-out dog shit littered the area, along with a few fresh clumps.

I picked up the petrified chunks first, saving the mushy ones for last. Finally, I was done. I tied the large plastic bag tightly and set it by the door. I glared at Django. "Don't you dare poop again today."

His mouth was open in a toothy doggy grin as he panted in the sun.

I brushed off a cushion under the pergola near where Dante sat and plopped down, stretching my legs out of the shade into the sun.

Dante leaned forward and clasped his hands together. "I got you a present."

"What? Why?"

"Just open it, baby," Darling said. I narrowed my eyes. She was in on this, too?

"I know when I was having a hard time dealing with Matt's death, the thing that saved me was getting far away from home and all the memories of him."

We were both silent for a second.

Matt had been killed at their wedding. A lunatic intent on killing me had instead taken out Matt and Bobby. Eventually, I got vengeance, but it didn't ease the agony of knowing the two men we'd loved were dead because of me.

Another reason not to fall in love ever again. I was deadly.

Dante and I rarely talked about Matt and Bobby. It had been nearly a year, but it was still too soon.

He stood with his back to me and continued talking. "It took a long time, but eventually I found I could go back and not want to cry every time I looked at something that reminded me of him."

I could feel tears welling in my eyes. Fuck.

Darling looked away.

"But you didn't ever do that," he said, turning to me. His eyes were hidden behind dark glasses. "You came back here right away."

"So?"

"You never had time to heal."

"No such thing."

"You have to try."

"Maybe I don't want to."

"I get that. I know you, Gia. And that's why I think you need to do something. For me."

I was instantly suspicious. He paced-looking out over the city as he spoke.

"Do what?"

"Take off. Go on a little vacation far away and do nothing except pamper yourself. Concentrate on healing."

"Whatever. I don't need to waste time doing that."

Darling rolled her eyes and Dante laughed so loud it startled me. "Waste time? What do you think you're doing now?"

"I meet with the board once a week and check my emails once a day."

He flung his arm out dismissing my claims of business as the nonsense they were.

"I want you to take a vacation and then come back and kick ass at work. You've got all these investors ready to tear the door down to get a piece of the action, and the board is freaking out, saying they can't get you to commit. They can't even count on you to show up once a week. You need to get on board. Take charge of this company or let someone else take the reins."

I frowned. I didn't want to deal with the company right now, but I also didn't want to turn it over. It was the last vestige of the empire my father had created, nurtured, and loved.

And I hated to admit it, but when I immersed myself in work for my father's company, I felt like I had a purpose. If I were honest, the work I'd done for the company—designing innovative developments where homeless people both worked and lived—was the most rewarding thing I'd ever done in my life.

My father must have known that putting me in charge of the company would magically transform me from drunken dilettante to proficient businesswoman practically overnight.

At first it did. Then Bobby was murdered. Now I was back to loser.

Dante leaned forward and handed me an envelope.

"The vacation is on me."

I pushed his hand away. "No."

"It's rude and disrespectful to refuse a gift given in love from a friend."

"Okay, fine," I grumbled, but opened the envelope.

I read the piece of paper. Dante had bought me airfare to Paris and a two-week Mediterranean cruise that took off from Barcelona, hit a few spots in Spain, spent a few days in Morocco, and ended in Portugal.

I made a face.

"What?"

"A cruise? Seriously? Cruises are for old people. Fake tourists. Lazy people. People who would rather eat than sightsee.

Dante shook his head. "You are a snob."

"Mmmm hmmm," Darling said with her lips pressed tightly together.

"No, I'm not." I was indignant.

"Yeah, you are."

"Whatever." I tossed the envelope on the end table beside me.

"If you feel like you're slumming, you can pay the difference and stay in the penthouse. It goes for a cool two-hundred-fifty."

"Two-hundred-fifty?"

"Two hundred and fifty thousand."

"For a fucking coffin-sized room on a floating death trap?"

"I doubt it is coffin-sized. Nor a death trap."

He crouched in front of me, putting his hands on mine. "Gia? Take the goddamn cruise. The reason I decided on this—and believe me, I thought long and hard about the perfect vacation for you—is because on a cruise you won't have to think."

He stood and clawed at his hair in frustration. "Gia. Look at you. You are a mess. You smell. You're a goddamn skeleton. Your skin is yellow. Hell, the whites of your eyes are yellow. You have dreadlocks whether you want them or not."

True.

"The cruise is perfect for you. It's a painless way for you to re-immerse yourself in the world. It will be slow and easy living. Your meals are provided. Your room is cleaned. I've arranged a laundry service. You eat and drink and sunbathe by the pool. If you want, you can get off at the stops and actually live a little."

"What stops?" I peered down. There were some pretty damn cool excursions: old caves, Casablanca, swimming with the dolphins. Okay, it didn't sound so bad.

"Will you go? For me?" He gave me the look. The look he'd given me since we were ten years old. The look that always got him his way.

"Fine." I shrugged.

"The only thing I ask is that you promise me you won't spend the entire trip in bed There's a shitload of things to do onboard. I spent a lot of money on this cruise to get your ass out of bed."

"*Capisco.*" I said it begrudgingly, because I knew what I'd just done. Made a promise I wouldn't break. Dante knew I would never lie to him and that I kept my word.

He stood and headed for the door back downstairs. Panic coursed through me. I'd just promised something that I didn't want to do. Every fiber of my being balked at a cruise. Even stepping foot out of my loft seemed impossible right now.

"Wait," I called after him. "I just remembered. I can't go."

He paused but didn't turn around. "Pray tell, why not?"

"Django," I said as if it were obvious. "I can't leave him."

"Thanh-Thanh has agreed to look after him while you're gone."

Shit.

He turned back toward me. "You're burning daylight. Get in the shower. Your plane leaves in three hours."

"What?" I practically screamed the word. I watched his back disappear down the stairs. But then I smiled. He knew if he gave me any time to think about it, I would change my mind.

3

WOMAN IN BLACK

Dante was smart to have me layover in Paris for two days.
But he'd also made a huge mistake because I was never coming home.

San Francisco was lovely, but this was fucking Paris, bitches.

Each morning I'd wake in my little pied-à-terre, open my eyes, turn my head to the left, and drink in the spectacular view of the motherfucking Eiffel Tower.

Then, while I was still in bed, there would be a little knock on the door, and some cute French waiter dude would bring me a croissant and coffee (okay, disclaimer—San Francisco's coffee is way better, but that's about the only thing I'd miss.)

I'd take my coffee out onto the little balcony, put my feet up on the wrought iron railing, and write in my journal. The leather-bound journal and Cross pen Dante had slipped me at the airport had been a life saver.

He'd pressed it into my hands and said, "Do me a favor, write about Bobby. Write about you. Write about your mother and dad. Or just play tic tac toe, but try to open this every day. I swear it will help."

I'd first opened it on the plane. I stared at the blank page. After two glasses of wine, I began to write. And couldn't stop.

I didn't dare go back and read my scribbles, but suffice it to say, it had a lot of "poor me" passages. But for some reason writing it all down felt good. Damn good.

Now I actually looked forward to writing in it every morning.

That morning I wrote about the man I saw at the hotel bar the night before. He was so mysterious. He was young and smoking hot, and he didn't even give me a second glance. At first, I was a little put out but then found it refreshing. Imagine my surprise when a sophisticated older woman in her late forties swooped up in a cloud of perfume. He dropped everything and kissed her palm and was attentive to her every need. Holy shit. Was he a gigolo? But then I saw the look on his face. He worshipped her. They left together, and I gawked in astonishment.

Some dude sitting beside me at the bar smirked.

"What?"

"You are American?"

I shrugged. It was obvious.

"You are surprised by that couple?"

I shrugged again.

"In Paris, we prefer women with experience. The confidence of an older woman," he put his fingers to his lips and kissed them. "The sexiest thing imaginable."

He was right. Older women in Paris had it going on.

I nodded. "Yeah, she was sexy as fuck."

He grinned.

"Don't get me wrong," he said, and put his hand on mine. "We like sexy younger women, too."

I pulled my hand out from his. "I'm sure."

I stood and left.

Now, I wrote about the encounter and smiled. When I hit fifty, I was moving to Paris. Maybe sooner. Who knew? I put the journal down and stretched. I was going shopping in the Le Marais and then later that afternoon, I'd board the train to Barcelona where I would catch my cruise ship the following day. I was looking forward to the overnight train ride. I loved trains. Well, I loved the idea of them. I hadn't actually *been* on one before. That's why Dante insisted I take the train.

He didn't miss a thing in planning this trip.

I'd take the cruise and then come back to Paris to live. I'd eat croissants every day, stroll the Luxembourg gardens, spend entire days at the *Louvre* and then party at the clubs in the Oberkampf district until dawn. And in twenty years, when I was a woman of a certain age, I'd find a young stud to keep me entertained.

First to get this damn cruise out of the way.

Sitting around with people who were too lazy—or too afraid—to tour a country the proper way. Not my thing. But if it made Dante happy, I'd give it a crack.

WEARING MY BIGGEST, blackest sunglasses, I surveyed the other passengers waiting to board the Stella Windstar cruise ship.

A lot of old, stuffy, snobby people showing off their fancy brands. Hermes. Prada. Louis Vuitton. Dior. Chanel. Just what I suspected: lazy, rich, probably snobby, too.

Whatev. What a waste.

Then, I heard tinkling laughter. All heads turned.

Down at the other end of the dock leading to our platform, a redheaded woman clinging to an older man was laughing.

Finally, someone my own age.

She was stunning. Tall, lean, silky red hair that fell straight down her back. Amber eyes, full lips, and cheekbones that could cut diamonds.

Wearing a silky, flowing white pantsuit, she made her way up the gangplank to the wide platform where we all waited to board. Everyone stopped to watch. Although her outfit was not revealing, she clearly didn't have a shirt on underneath the deep-cut lapels of the white blazer.

The distinguished man at her side was dressed as her mirror image, in a black linen suit. His full mane of hair swept back and was mostly gray. He was probably in his sixties. She was clearly in her twenties. I would've thought the man was her grandfather until she leaned over and kissed his mouth with her voluptuous pink lips for so long the gawking crowd shifted uncomfortably.

Once they reached the platform where we waited to board, people pretended not to stare. The red-haired woman talked excitedly to the man in a low voice. He grinned down at her indulgently. She held tightly to his hand, squeezing it with enthusiasm. She exclaimed and stretched up on tiptoe to kiss him again, this time pressing her body against him.

He said something to her and she laughed—that tinkling sound again.

Then she focused on me, and her mouth spread in a wide smile. She stuck her hand out to me.

"Natasha Ainsley." Her voice had a slight accent that I couldn't place.

Her smile was contagious. I smiled back and took her hand.

"Gia Santella."

Shooting a glance at the older people surrounding us, she spoke in a low voice. "Happy to see someone my age here. We are going to have so much fun together. I think you're my type of woman, Gia Santella."

I was at little taken aback by how forward she was, but also secretly pleased.

We sat there grinning like fools at one another.

Just then, four massive SUV's pulled up and a few dozen people our age showed up.

"Thank God," Natasha said, reading my mind. We wouldn't be the only people in our twenties aboard. She winked at me. "Let's get this party started!"

She leaned over to me. "Are you into the Marvel Universe? You know, like *The Avengers*?"

I blinked. What the hell was she talking about? "Isn't Marvel a comic book company?"

"Yes. TV and movies, too. Superhero stuff."

What was she? Twelve? I shrugged. "Sorry, no."

"What?" She drew back and looked at me with wide eyes. "Okay. Well, you look like one of The Defenders characters, Jessica Jones. You kind of remind me of her, too—your voice, your mannerisms."

"Okay," I said and lit a cigarette. "Cool."

She eyed my cigarette hungrily, so I held out my pack. Her eyes flitted to her husband. "No, thanks. I don't smoke."

But then she gave me a slow wink.

I smiled.

The younger group boarded the walkway

They were obviously Greek or Italian or Spanish. Men with black curly hair and blinding white smiles. Women with startling blue eyes against bronzed skin. Young. Sexy. Rich.

One man, at the front of the group, leaned back against the rail casually, facing Natasha and me. Slowly, he lifted his sunglasses, and his eyes roved my body. He ogled me nakedly, starting at my stiletto sandals and raking his gaze over me.

I watched him coolly, waiting for his eyes to reach mine. When they did, I lifted one eyebrow, stared pointedly at his crotch, and ran my tongue over my lips.

It had the desired effect. He quickly looked away.

Natasha, who had observed the entire subtle exchange, burst into tinkly laughter.

"We're going to get along just fine."

The smile on her face faded. She was looking over my shoulder toward the shore. Her cheeks blossomed pink.

"What is *she* doing here?" Her voice was low and vicious.

Turning, I saw a woman step onto the gangplank, flanked by two men pulling luggage racks stacked with suitcases. Even from here I could make out the Louis Vuitton logos. The woman wore a tight black dress, high-heeled black pumps and had her hair pulled back in a bun. She wore huge Jackie-O-style sunglasses. As she grew closer, I saw that she was older, maybe in her forties or fifties, it was hard to tell.

I shot a glance at Natasha. She was leaning over whispering to her husband. His brow was furrowed and he seemed to be trying to calm her down. The only words I could make out were him saying, "I have no idea."

Before the woman in black reached us, Natasha tugged on Henry's arm and pulled him to the front of the line waiting to board, pushing past other people. The captain released the red rope separating us from the ship, and the minor stampede to board began.

4

HAIR OF THE DOG

I lost track of Natasha and the woman in black as I boarded.

A man in white approached me immediately, introduced himself, and then guided me to my cabin.

My clothes had already been unpacked. My sandals and dresses were all neatly displayed in the closet. My stash of booze was lined up on the dresser, along with a welcome basket of dates, oranges, and grapes alongside a plate of gold-wrapped Godiva chocolates. A shelf above the headboard was filled with brand new candles in frosted glass containers.

The suite was insanely luxurious and yet comfortable and inviting at the same time.

I flopped on the bed, overwhelmed by loneliness and grief. I couldn't help but imagine walking into this cabin suite with Bobby. I'd take his hand, lead him to the bed and undress him, kiss every inch of him, and then spend the rest of the day making love to him. We would emerge for the formal dinner, our faces flushed, our bodies still tender. Everyone would look at us and know—and not only because I'd have that freshly-fucked look—makeup a little smeared, hair a little messy, a languid, sleepy contentment suffusing every inch of my body.

But no.

I was here in this cabin by myself. I poured some bourbon, gulped it down, and then poured another few fingers into the crystal glass. I repeated it until a fuzzy glow overcame me. I flopped on my back and stared at the ceiling, denying that the wetness sliding down my cheeks was tears. I woke curled in the fetal position, shivering from the aggressive air conditioning with the setting sun coating everything in the cabin with a surreal orange glow.

My head pounded. At first I reached for my bag to unearth some pills, but then I thought, "Fuck it. I'm going full hair-of-the-dog on this trip." I turned up the thermostat to seventy-seven degrees, poured another drink, and brought it into the shower with me. I stood under the pounding water and sipped my drink until I felt halfway normal again.

When I was done with my shower, I peered into the closet.

What I wanted to do was pull on my soft and worn-in leather pants and a cozy sweater, but the dinner invitation that had been slipped under my door said formal wear was required.

I tugged on an ankle-length black dress with spaghetti straps. It had a deep scoop neck, but revealed no cleavage. The back of the dress dipped down to my lower back, revealing a long slice of my spine, but nothing inappropriate. It would do. I slipped on long dangling emerald earrings that had been my mothers, two slashes of Kohl eyeliner and called it a win.

The dining room was like a Titanic scene. A sweeping staircase deposited us in the room. Women wore floor-length, bedazzled gowns with white gloves. Are you fucking kidding me? And men wore tuxedos. Armani, no doubt.

Another white-coated attendant took my arm. "Miss Santella, I will escort you to your seat."

I gave him a double take. How did he know my name? He led me to a table at the rear of the room where I saw Natasha and her husband already seated.

Henry rose and kissed both my cheeks. Natasha pulled out the chair beside her. "Please sit by me!" She leaned over and whispered, "I asked for them to seat you at our table. I hope you don't mind?"

I was flattered, but didn't know how to answer so I simply smiled.

It felt strange, but also good to have someone want my company. I can't say that it's always been that way in my life. Especially when it came to women my age. Most of the time, they liked me to sit far, far away from their husband or boyfriends, which always confused me, since the last thing I was into was home-wrecking.

Natasha was turned toward me, talking, but kept her hand behind her holding Henry's. Every once in a while, she would turn to him and kiss him on the cheek.

"Are you a newlywed?" I asked, eyes narrowing.

Her laugh was infectious. "Hardly. Six months now. But to be honest, I feel like a newlywed. Henry treats me like a princess. I'm so lucky."

When the waiter brought a plate of sushi as an appetizer, Natasha plucked one off the communal plate for Henry and then passed the plate to me.

"You don't like sushi? I'll eat yours."

She smiled. "I normally do, but ..." She gestured to her abdomen.

It took me a few seconds to get it. "Oh," I said. "Oh. Are you... are you...?"

Her cheeks flushed a pretty pink. "We're trying."

But then she grew somber and said in a low voice, "It's been six months. I'm heartbroken it's taking so long. That's why Henry took me on this cruise. I was depressed. The doctor said maybe the stress of trying and having nothing happen was causing nothing to happen."

I nodded. I didn't know much about trying to get knocked up— since I'd spent my entire adult life trying *not* to get that way—but I plastered a sympathetic look on my face.

I eyed her glass of wine. She lifted her chin, haughtily. "In France, all pregnant women drink."

I didn't know if that was true or not, but it seemed like another good reason to move to Paris.

Henry cleared his throat and she brightened. Whether it was fake or not I didn't know, but she smiled and took Henry's arm.

"I have the most marvelous plan," she said. "Henry and I discussed it this afternoon. There are so many excursions I want to take on this cruise, but right before we left, Henry's doctor said he should probably sit most of them out. We are visiting some friends of Henry's in Ibiza. But for the other excursions, I was wondering if you might want to go with me. To keep me company. You don't already have your excursions planned, do you? The last time to sign up is tomorrow morning. If you go with me, we'll pay for the excursions, won't we, sugar?"

Henry nodded, lifting an eyebrow.

"That sounds great," I said. "On one condition—I pay my own way."

Natasha pouted.

"I insist."

Henry met my eyes and nodded. "Fair enough."

Natasha took out the brochure of excursions from her bag, and we spread it over the table.

"This sounds phenomenal." I pointed to an excursion to explore St. Michael's Cave in Gibraltar. "Want to do this one?"

She hesitated and then smiled. "Um, sure. I'm a little freaked out by underground, but maybe it will be okay."

Henry laughed. "It'll be fine. It's as big as a house inside."

"If you say so, honey," she said and squeezed his arm.

Natasha mentioned wanting to swim with the dolphins in Gibraltar while we were there, and I readily agreed.

"It looks like we get there early morning and don't leave until close to midnight. We can do both."

Then I spotted the tour of Tangier and Casablanca. "This one looks like fun." I held the brochure up to Natasha.

She paused. Her brow furrowed. She didn't answer.

Henry said, "You talked about wanting to do that when I first mentioned the cruise." He chuckled. "I can't believe you didn't pick that one first."

She shifted and looked down. "When is that again?

"Second to last port—right before Lisbon."

Her mouth formed a small circle. "Oh. For some reason, I'd thought it was one of the early stops. It doesn't matter, though." Then she smiled. "Yes, yes, let's sign up for that one, too. For sure. Silly me. That's been my dream since I was little."

Henry said, "I can't believe you'd even hesitate. That was one reason I picked this cruise line."

She looked distressed. She pinched her lips tightly together, and her cheeks blossomed red.

"Darling?" Henry took her hand in his.

She exhaled. "I guess I feel guilty. I thought maybe one day I could just stay on board with you, and we could hang by the pool. When we talked about going to Casablanca, I'd thought we could go together. I didn't know your stuffy doctor would restrict you to the ship. I would feel so badly leaving you here alone." She seemed sheepish.

"Nonsense!" Henry said heartily. "You and Gia are going to do that excursion. No debate."

She smiled, but it was still a tight smile. "Okay. I'll be sure to sign us up at the desk first thing in the morning."

"I'll meet you there," I said.

I noticed her features darken, but she was looking at a group at another table. The woman in black was holding court. All heads were turned toward her. I could barely make out her voice, but she said something, held up her wine glass, and everyone burst into laughter and applause. Without the large sunglasses that had hid her face earlier, I could see she was beautiful in an Isabella Rossellini-type way.

"Is she Italian?" I said to Natasha.

My new friend looked at me with wide, horrified eyes. I realized I'd made a major faux pas bringing up the woman in her presence.

Natasha quickly gulped down her wine and then turned toward Henry. She slipped her hand into his lap and I was certain it was to make sure his attention was fully on her.

When the waiter brought Henry's plate, Natasha scraped the au gratin potatoes off onto a small plate. She did the same with hers. "We need to watch your cholesterol, Henry. Maybe we can have some for lunch tomorrow, but let's skip it for tonight, okay?"

Henry didn't disagree. Why would he? She made it sound so reasonable.

Henry winked at me. "She's always careful about what I eat. Keeping me on track. Says she wants to keep me around a while."

"That shouldn't be a problem," I said. "What are you fifty?"

It elicited the desired laughter I'd hoped for.

"Add two decades onto that," he said.

I widened my eyes in surprise. "You're kidding?"

Later, after the waiter cleared our dessert plates and Henry stood, waiting by her chair.

I glanced over at the other table, but the woman in black was already gone.

"Let's hang out tonight," Natasha said, lacing her fingers through mine. I pulled my hand away. I wasn't used to her affection. It made me slightly uncomfortable. "Henry is an old fuddy-duddy and goes to bed early. But I'm ready to party. Let's go hit the club. We can dance until we drop."

Henry laughed and leaned over to kiss her brow. "Have fun, you two."

As soon as Henry left, Natasha leaned toward me with a wicked gleam in her eyes. "Got any of those cigarettes?"

On the Riviera Deck, we stood outside, leaning against the rail, smoking.

"What's up with that woman? The one in black?" I said.

"Long story. She and Henry had a thing once. She always manages to pop up wherever we are. They still share the same circle of friends, so I have to see her everywhere: Cannes. Rio. Aspen. St. Tropez. I don't know how she possibly knew we were taking this cruise. She's such a witch. She's only here to make my life hell."

"That sucks," I said.

"Tell me about it." She exhaled an expert stream of smoke in front of us that drifted out over the dark sea below. Not a smoker, my ass.

"Let's not talk about her," she said. "Let's talk about you. Why are you here alone, Giada Valentina Santella?"

"Long story," I said, repeating her own words.

"Give me the Cliff Notes."

"My boyfriend died last year. My gay best friend thought this cruise would help me get over it."

"Oh my God. I'm so sorry." She blinked rapidly. Was she crying?

For some reason, I didn't want to tell her that Bobby had been murdered. I wasn't sure why.

Natasha leaned over, arching her neck toward me to see my face.

"Oh, Gia. How awful."

Her breast was touching my bare arm. She left it there. I wasn't sure if it was an accident or on purpose, but I moved away. It's not that I've never imagined being with a woman. I mean, women are sexy. But right now, I had quite a few objections to being hit on by my new friend. For one, Natasha was married.

Shit like that counts for me.

I may have slept around a little—okay, a lot. But once I committed to monogamy, that was it.

In addition, I didn't need someone else to have sex with. God knows that's never been a problem for me. What I really needed was a friend. A platonic friend. A homegirl. Darling was right.

Sex always fucked up friendships. Period.

Natasha must have sensed my thoughts, because she backed off. She flicked her cigarette butt into the sea below us.

I made a face. "That's classy."

Her eyes widened. "You're right. Nobody should litter. I'm such an awful person. Please forgive me." She took my hand again in hers. "I've been hanging out with a douchey crowd in Cannes for too long. They are pigs when you think about it. I've developed some terribly horrendous habits as a result. I'm sorry. I need more friends like you."

I forgave her.

"Let's go find that club. I need to move," I said.

The Star Bar was a club at one end of the Baja Deck. It had low ceilings, low lighting, and lots of sweaty bodies. The dance floor was packed. It looked like the entire crowd of Greek young people were there, plus some other people I'd never seen who must have boarded after us. The ship held 300 people so there were most definitely new faces. I made a point to dance with the cutest ones. The DJ was good, and Natasha and I danced for three hours before we both slumped, exhausted, in a corner booth.

"God, I needed that," I said to her. "Thanks."

Gulping her third glass of water in as many minutes, Natasha pushed back her damp bangs and yawned. "Me, too. We should do this every night. Plus, it'll help burn off the calories from all this rich food."

I laughed.

"What?"

"Don't worry about shit like that."

She eyed me. "Well, you probably don't have to."

I shrugged.

"If I had your curves, I wouldn't worry as much, either. But any weight I gain goes to my gut. Not attractive."

"Shut up. You are fucking gorgeous."

"I agree." A voice said. I looked up. A blond woman stood over our table.

She was petite and curvy and wore a silver tank top and tight black leggings. She had big blue eyes and dimples.

"Do you want to dance?" She ignored me. She was speaking to Natasha.

I watched Natasha take the woman in and then smile. "Well," she hesitated and looked at me.

"I'm beat," I said. "I'm heading to bed."

Natasha hesitated for a second and then said, "Me, too. Thanks anyway."

As we walked out, I glanced back and saw the woman on the dance floor doing a slow sexy dance. Her eyes were on Natasha.

5

YOU CAN'T COMPETE WITH A DEAD WOMAN

L ying in the dark in my ridiculously comfortable bed in my luxurious suite, I examined my feelings as I started to drift off to sleep. Lying in bed before I fell asleep was the witching hour for me. It was always the most difficult time of the day. I often tried to find that line between buzzed enough to not let my grief overcome me and so shit-faced I just wept until morning and had no control in blocking thoughts of Bobby.

Tonight, I was surprised to realize I wasn't grief-stricken. I was melancholy, yes. I was lonely, yes. But sometime tonight, I'd latched onto a nearly forgotten feeling: hope and anticipation. This new friendship with Natasha had given me a reason to look forward to waking up in the morning.

I was up early and threw on a navy, sleeveless sundress, leather flip flops, and huge, dark sunglasses and headed for the front desk. On the way, I peered out the window. We'd arrived in Ibiza earlier.

Brilliant turquoise seas were scattered with sailboat masts. Beyond the shore lay a hillside jam-packed with squared, white-washed buildings dotted with dark windows. From the sea, it looked like all the buildings were right on top of one another.

All I knew of Ibiza was that it was the party playground to celebrities, but I was willing to check it out.

Once at the front desk, I examined the brochure again. Natasha appeared at my side.

"Oh good, you're up." She squeezed my elbow and then let her fingernails trail down my arm. Vaguely, I remembered her brushing her breast up against my bare arm last night and wondered again if it was just a coincidence.

Either way, I was happy for her company on this ship.

After we signed up for the excursions, Natasha turned to me.

"I was hoping you'd come ashore with Henry and me today. Some of his old friends invited us to their villa for lunch and a swim. They are Henry's friends from forever ago and knew his deceased wife, so I'm a little nervous. Every time I meet friends he had when he was married before, I feel like they're judging me. They never give me a chance. You can't compete with a dead woman, you know."

"Yeah, I bet that sucks."

"She was apparently pretty amazing," Natasha said, as we walked over to the rail to take in Ibiza. "A human rights attorney. Traveled to Chernobyl to help people. Worked with lepers. Blah. Blah. Blah. And beautiful. I can't compete. I'm just some dumb twenty-five-year-old who grew up in the Ukraine and doesn't even have a college degree."

"Stop that. You're smart and fun and gorgeous," I said.

"You'd be doing me a favor if you came along. I wouldn't feel so awkward and out of sorts."

"Sure." My quick response surprised me. But I couldn't help it, I wanted to spend time with Natasha. Another woman had never sought out my friendship like this before. It felt good.

She leaned over and kissed my cheek, close to my mouth. "Meet us at eleven at the Aloha Deck. That's where we disembark."

"Deal."

As I walked away, a small part of me wondered about the breast brushing and the trailing fingers and the kiss near my mouth. But then again, maybe all women were affectionate like this with their friends. How the fuck would I know? I'd never had a friend like this before.

At eleven, I showed up on deck still in my sundress, but had added a black straw fedora and black woven basket to use as a bag. Inside, I'd tucked my turquoise bikini, a small rolled up Turkish towel, a joint, and a small flask, in case the party got boring.

The villa was fantastic. Perched on a cliff side overlooking the water. The far end of the pool sported a massive concrete arch framing a spectacular view of the sea below.

The partygoers clustered together, catching up, while Natasha and I headed to the pool. As Natasha had mentioned, most of the women were older, closer to Henry's age. They wore filmy caftans over their swimsuits and slides with kitten heels as they pranced around the pool holding martini glasses high and nibbling on small canapes being proffered by three handsome waiters.

Natasha and I staked out comfy lounge chairs by the pool. I sipped on a fruity cocktail that one of the cute waiters had handed me and then lay flat, pulling my hat over my eyes. The sun soaking into my skin was just the healing I needed. Sometimes I wondered why the hell I even lived in foggy San Francisco. My Italian body craved the warmth of the sun. It was pure medicine.

"This is heavenly," I said.

Natasha didn't answer. I sat up. She'd fallen asleep on her stomach. Her pale skin was turning a little pink. I looked for Henry. He was deep in conversation with a group of men. The circle of women, staked out a table under an umbrella, occasionally shot looks our way. Fuck 'em.

I draped my Turkish towel over Natasha's back, trying not to wake her, but she sat up sleepily.

"Sorry," I said. "I was worried you'd burn."

"Oh my God. Yes. How silly of me. I didn't mean to fall asleep." She stretched languidly. "I didn't get much sleep last night."

She blushed.

"Really?" I said, and winked. "Don't make me jealous. I'm here solo."

"Ha. You won't be for long." She took a long sip of her drink. "Henry may be older, but with help from his little blue pills, he is a most excellent lover."

I remembered what she'd said about not being able to get pregnant yet. Obviously, it had nothing to do with Henry's sexual prowess.

"Good for you."

She giggled, that same tinkling, infectious laugh. The women and the men all turned and looked. I raised my glass to them in a toast, and they all turned away again—the men smiling, and the women rolling their eyes.

"Listen," Natasha leaned forward and grabbed my hand. "I'm awfully sorry about your boyfriend. Have you had sex since then?"

I stared at her, unsure how to answer. I didn't want to lie and tell her no, but I wasn't sure she needed to know the extent of my debauchery in that department. Plus, it *had* been a while. I'd been holed up solitary in my loft for weeks.

I settled on shrugging.

"I can tell. You need to get laid."

I had no idea what made her think that, but I figured her assessment was right. When I didn't protest, she smiled.

"Okay then, it's settled. Let's find you a lover for this trip. I saw quite a few eligible men on board. They were all at the pool this morning, working on their tans."

"The Greek boys?"

"Yes!" she exclaimed. "Not for a relationship but an onboard fling, Perfect."

"Yeah, you might be right. No strings attached. Just great sex."

She settled back into her chair. "It's settled then. Tonight, we hit the bar after dinner and find you a lover. Don't worry, I'll help. I used to slay at that. I could probably dig up some old tricks."

I nodded. I didn't tell her that was one area where I'd never needed any help.

A commotion near the sliding glass door to the house made me sit up at the same time Natasha gasped.

It was that woman in black. She wore a black maxi sundress and a man's fedora. She was barefoot and carried a straw bag. I envied her effortless chic.

Natasha groaned beside me. "I was hoping for one day without her around."

I kept my eyes plastered on Henry. He didn't seem ruffled, but he also didn't seem overly interested in the woman's sudden appearance, either.

"What's Henry think of her stalking you guys?" I said.

"He says she's harmless, but he's also such a good guy, he doesn't see how evil she really is."

Evil.

"Why do you say that?"

"She's the black widow."

I sat up. "Explain."

Natasha reached for her drink. "Her last husband disappeared. Poof. Vanished one day. She inherited all his fortune, which was quite substantial."

"Her last husband?"

"Yeah, he was number five or something."

"Give me the scoop," I said.

"I'm going to need to be more drunk to spend more than a nanosecond talking about her, but I don't want to refill my glass."

We both eyed the bar, which was just beyond where the woman stood in the center of the group of women.

"I've got a better idea," I said.

Rummaging in my basket, I found a joint I'd bought onshore in Barcelona and my pink plastic lighter. I put the joint between my lips and jutted my chin toward the group in the shade. "You think they'll object?"

Natasha took the lighter out of my hands and lit the end of the joint. "I don't give a fuck."

We spent the rest of the afternoon dozing and giggling and taking dips in the pool. The other women stayed in the shade, gathered around a table talking. Fine by me.

I'd managed to avoid meeting the woman in black until it was time to return to the ship. We wanted to make it back in time for the eight o'clock dinner hour because we'd be dining at the captain's table.

At that point, everyone had moved inside and we followed. Natasha went ahead of me and disappeared down a hallway with Henry. I stood there, awkwardly.

The woman in black came over and extended her hand.

"I don't think we've met," she said with a smile. "I'm Sharon Long."

"Gia Santella." I took her hand firmly.

"You are a new friend of the Ainsley's?" Her blue eyes were probing and didn't match her warm smile.

It took me a minute to realize she was referring to Henry and Natasha. I nodded.

"Well, any friend of Henry's is a friend of mine." This time her smile reached her eyes.

I was taken aback. She was charming. But my loyalty was to my new friend, so I gave a small smile. "Nice to meet you. If you'll excuse me."

Taking off down the hall, I found Natasha and Henry in the dark in an embrace.

"Sorry." I backed away.

Natasha laughed. "Oh, good. I was just going to go find you. Our driver is outside."

We piled into the town car that would take us back to the ship. Henry was in good spirits. And for good reason. Natasha stuck her hand in his lap and groped him right in front of me. His eyes were glazed. He was drunk and grinning like a fool. I tried to look out the window to give them some privacy, but before it got too hot and heavy, we were at the dock where a small boat would take us to our ship.

Once we were aboard, Natasha and Henry probably didn't even hear me say goodbye as they headed to their cabin, stopping to kiss every few feet.

"See you at dinner," I said lamely to their backs.

Natasha was right. It was time for me to take a new lover.

6

FIRE NEEDS OXYGEN

At dinner, Natasha and I got to sit on either side of the captain, a distinguished looking German man with gray hair and moustache, a ready smile, and a military bearing.

I scanned the dining room. The woman in black, Sharon Long, was nowhere to be seen.

After we received some tiny toasts with pate to munch on before the main course, Natasha leaned forward and addressed the captain.

"Captain, please don't think I'm a big baby, but I have an irrational fear of fire and being on board a ship in the middle of the ocean is a little bit out of my comfort zone."

Henry, on her other side, widened his eyes. "Oh my, darling, I didn't even think. You should've said something."

She put her hand on his arm. "I didn't want you to cancel the trip. It's fine."

The captain smiled. "It's a logical question and a reasonable concern. We have a few methods to contain the spread of fire onboard. Most of our compartments, especially ones that are vital to the functioning of the ship, such as the engine room and the communications room, are airtight so they can be sealed off from the rest of the ship in the event of a fire."

Natasha blinked. "But if the engine room burns up, we still are in trouble, no?"

"Yes," he said. "But within the airtight chambers—and in all suites and cabins, basically every room onboard—we have a series of stop-gap measures to put the fire out automatically. Sensors triggered from smoke will activate the system. It extinguishes the fire in two ways. The first is through the traditional method of sprinklers. At the same time, we have a superb, high-tech manner to fight the fire."

"You've got my attention," I said and took another sip of my wine without taking my eyes off of him.

"Researchers in Denmark discovered a crystalline substance stemming from cobalt that will suck all the oxygen out of the air. And as you know, fire needs oxygen to live."

"This substance drops, along with the water from the sprinklers into the room. It is invisible to the naked eye, but even a teaspoon of it absorbs all the oxygen in a good-size room."

"Fascinating," I said and looked at Natasha. She winked.

"And that's not the half of it," the captain said.

Natasha leaned forward, eyes glassy. "All the oxygen is sucked out of the room, you say?"

The captain nodded. She sat back.

"What is particularly interesting about this substance is not that such a small amount of it can hold so much oxygen—although that is quite remarkable in itself. The part that is exciting to me, is it not only-holds and contains the oxygen, but it does not damage it, and with heat and other methods, the oxygen can be released from the crystalline substance and return to its original molecular form."

"Huh?" I was contemplating the potential of that when the captain held up a finger.

"This means that people, say, who currently need oxygen in a big tank, could carry just a small mask. How interesting is that?"

I smiled widely at his enthusiasm.

Just then Henry leaned in. "Say, what's the name of the company that discovered the crystalline substance? I bet it would be something my firm will want to look into."

I tuned out the rest of the conversation. The last thing I wanted to think about was venture capitalism. I knew that ball of wax was waiting for me back at home in San Francisco. I'd deal with it then. I was on vacation.

After the captain excused himself and the dessert plates were cleared, Natasha kissed Henry on the cheek. "Go smoke that fancy cigar I bought you. Gia and I are going to go change and then head to the club to dance. Don't wait up, lover. It's going to be a late one. We're finding Gia a beau."

He chuckled and gave me a kiss on the cheek. "I doubt you'll have any trouble with that."

The smile I gave him was genuine. He was such a sweet man. He obviously doted on Natasha and made her happy. He was filthy rich, though not pretentious, and so easygoing. He'd proven that with his uptight friends at the party. Natasha could do no wrong. He didn't give a shit what anyone else thought. He loved her. I needed a man like that. Maybe that attitude came with age. Maybe I'd been looking at men too young. Maybe an older, sophisticated man was the way to go. The captain was attractive with his power and intelligence and passion. But I wasn't quite ready to go for a gray-haired man just yet. One step at a time.

WHEN WE WALKED into the club this time, heads turned.

We'd shed our floor-length dinner gowns.

Natasha had changed into a white blazer with nothing underneath and a tight white miniskirt with sky-high heels. I wore a black silk shirt unbuttoned to *there* and a black leather skirt with strappy black heels.

Ignoring the stares, I headed to the bar with Natasha behind me.

I gulped my bourbon straight up and ordered another while Natasha sipped on a mojito.

They were the only drinks we would buy ourselves that night. The drinks and attention kept coming. A young Greek man with a regal nose begged Natasha to join him on the dance floor. She winked and gave me a kiss on the cheek before leaving.

The man's friend, another Greek with curly black hair, earnestly told me about how he'd dreamed of me the night before.

"I like your scar." He drew one finger down my cheekbone. Mention of my scar made me wince. Not because it marred my face, but because it was a constant reminder that an albino psycho was still out there somewhere, probably thinking of me.

But I smiled back at the boy even as I thought "think of something original."

He ordered another drink for me, and I eagerly sucked it down. It would take a lot of booze for me to stop thinking tonight. All I wanted was to feel. Not think.

By the time he switched to French, telling me how sexy I was, I felt no pain. His hand was on my bare thigh, and I liked it. He had girlish long, black eyelashes and sincere black eyes. His lips were pink and looked soft, so I leaned over and bit the lower one gently.

"*Eíste tóso séxi*," he said in Greek.

The only word I understood was "sexy." I pulled back and laughed.

"*Agapi mou. Se thelo! Anasa mou*," he said.

"I have no idea what you are saying."

"You know how to speak this, then, no?" He leaned over and kissed my neck.

"Oh, that language I do know."

He would do.

I searched for Natasha on the dark dance floor. I didn't see her white-clad figure among the grinding bodies. I wanted to tell her goodbye before I brought this boy back to my room.

He nibbled on my ear and tugged on my hand.

Turning, I searched the corners of the club. That's when I spotted her deep in a corner booth. I could only see her profile, her head tilted, kissing a blond woman. Natasha ran her fingers through the other woman's hair, pulling her close. Their faces appeared like snapshots as the dance floor's flickering strobe light periodically flashed on them. Then Natasha pulled away, and the blonde woman threw her head back against the velvet cushion of the booth and closed her eyes, mouth open. Natasha's hands were busy somewhere under the table.

I couldn't look away.

The Greek kissed my neck and stroked my thigh, his hand stretching higher by the second. I was ready to have sex right there, but... Natasha.

I turned back toward the boy. "Yes. One minute."

When I looked back toward the booth in the corner, it was empty.

Then I spotted them. Natasha had her hand on the woman's waist, guiding her out a side door. At the last minute, she glanced over and our eyes met. She looked down at the floor and then turned and left.

A few minutes later, the Greek and I were at my cabin.

After I let us in, he kneeled on the floor before me. As soon as his mouth met my thigh, I knew I'd made a good call. My body melted under his touch. I turned my brain and thoughts off completely and let my need take over. And I can't deny that images of Natasha and that woman fueled my lust into something undeniably primal.

A few hours later, I woke with a crazy thirst only to find the spot in bed beside me empty. Good. I vaguely remembered telling him he couldn't stay. He hadn't argued.

After downing two large glasses of water, I fell back to sleep.

I woke later to a text from Natasha.

"I'm so ashamed."

She should be.

Fuck who you want—*if* you are single. She was married.

In the cold light of day, her cheating didn't sit well with me.

I didn't want to judge her, but it did make me question my new friend's morals and values.

In my opinion, loyalty was possibly the most important trait in a person. I knew it stemmed from my Italian side, was probably buried deep in my DNA. Without loyalty, my Sicilian ancestors probably would've been murdered by outsiders. Holding family above all had kept our bloodline rich.

A wave of sadness and loneliness swept over me thinking about family. I had one relative left. An aunt. A rogue, badass, and knife-wielding Italian mob boss known as the Queen of Spades. I had her card, but it seemed weird to just call her. She didn't seem like the motherly type. I had memorized her number to use in an emergency.

Finally, I sat up in bed and texted Natasha back.

"Let's meet at the pool." It was an at-sea day.

7

MORALS OF AN ALLEY CAT

"I was drunk." It was the first thing she said to me poolside.

"What does Henry say about all this?"

"He doesn't know. He takes sleeping pills. Once he pops a pill, it's lights out until the next morning."

"Oh."

"You probably think I'm a monster, don't you?" She wore dark sunglasses so I couldn't see her eyes.

I didn't reply.

"Do you still want to go into Cartagena with me tomorrow?"

The one friend I'd made as an adult has the morals of an alley cat. Oh well. Not my problem. It's not like we were going to hang out all the time once this vacation was over. Natasha had told me they split their time between homes in Cannes and London.

But I had to admit my enthusiasm about our friendship had slightly waned.

～

THE FIRST STOP on our tapas tour in Cartagena was a dark Moorish restaurant where we each were allowed to order two glasses of wine and two tapas. The owner recommended *chopitos*, batter-fried baby squid, along with little toasts with goat's cheese and Iberian jam, so, of course, I agreed.

Natasha said in a dull voice, "I'll have the same."

But she only took small nibbles of each. I wasn't sure why she'd even wanted to go on this excursion. The same thing happened at the next restaurant, she picked at her food, taking maybe three bites and then ordered seconds on the wine. By that point, with four glasses of wine in her, she had loosened up a little. She turned to me with a smile.

"You're lucky. You don't have to watch your figure."

I finished shoving a huge hunk of chorizo in my mouth before I answered.

"I watch it just fine, but I'm not going to deprive myself. Especially around food like this on a trip like this. I'd rather eat delicious food than be size zero."

She scrunched up her face. "I've heard that before."

"Sophia Bush."

"Ah, yes. She's Italian?"

I pushed the plate of toast toward her. It was topped with caramelized onions and melted gorgonzola cheese.

"Live a little."

She shook her head and rolled her eyes, lifting her hand for another drink.

At the last stop, I discovered my favorite new drink ever: *Asiático* coffee, a heavenly mixture of liquor, coffee, cream, brandy, and cinnamon.

"Oh my god," I said. "You have to try this."

Since it was alcohol, she did.

The owner told us that the drink had been around for hundreds of years. Cartagena fishermen used to carry poor quality coffee, milk and brandy to drink while fishing to keep them warm, he said.

By the time, we got back to the ship, we were both drunk and giggling. Natasha had gotten over her glum mood, and I'd gotten over my judgmental nature.

I realized I'd been acting like a Class-A hypocrite. After all, I knew people judged me constantly because I liked sex, booze, and drugs. And wearing leather pants to the grocery store. Who was I to make up this lame-ass standard and look down on Natasha? Stupid.

On my deck, I stepped out of the elevator yawning. We'd agreed to nap in our respective cabins before dinner and made plans to return to the club that night after we ate. "But just to dance," Natasha said, looping her arm through mine. "Nothing else."

AFTER MY SHOWER, I threw on a clingy, navy silk dress with a deep scoop neck to wear to dinner. The dress fell to my ankles, and the sleeves reached to my wrists. I pulled my black hair back in a tight ponytail and slicked on red lipstick, foregoing any jewelry.

When I walked in, I paused at the foot of the stairs to the dining room as the maître d' took my arm and escorted me to my table. A familiar face caught my attention. The Greek boy toy from last night. I gave a long, slow wink, but he pointedly ignored me with a blank face and turned toward a woman poured into a sequined, pink dress to his right.

Of course.

Everybody had somebody.

Henry stood when I approached, pulling out my chair and greeting me with a kiss on the cheek. As he pushed in my chair, he leaned down and whispered. "Thanks for being a good friend to Natasha."

Once we'd settled in, I turned to him. "What did you do all day by your lonesome, Henry?" I asked.

"He worked," Natasha said, and rolled her eyes.

Henry laughed. "Someone's got to work to pay for all this."

Loud laughter erupted a few tables over and most people at our table turned to look, including me. I recognized the woman's black bun immediately. Sharon Long. Natasha stared straight ahead. I didn't blame her for not looking. Henry, God bless him, leaned in to

Natasha and rubbed his thumb along her wrist. She brightened immediately.

After dinner, Natasha and I skipped the club. Instead, we curled up on the deck by the swimming pool under thick cashmere blankets provide by the crew. We smoked and drank white wine.

Natasha looked up at something above me, smiled, and raised her glass. I glanced up. The top level of the ship was where the quarter-million dollar penthouses were. I saw Henry standing on the penthouse balcony in a silk bathrobe. He held up a glass to us in a salute and then disappeared.

"Is he spying on you?" I don't know why I said it, but the words slipped out.

"God, no. He's just being sweet and saying goodnight."

"Oh, I'm sorry."

"Don't apologize. I'm very lucky. Henry trusts me implicitly."

I shot a look at her.

"Yeah, well, I'm not fucking perfect. I'm young. I've slipped. But every time I do, I end up confessing. He knows I can't keep anything from him."

I thought about that for a few seconds.

"Does that mean you're going to tell him about last night?"

She exhaled loudly and then shrugged.

I let it go. What did I know about marriage? Nothing, that's what.

And Natasha obviously trusted him. Even with Henry's ex-lover on board, she had no qualms about leaving him alone on the ship. I admired and respected that sort of trust.

We smoked and sipped our *Asiaticos*. I'd taught the bartender on the Sun Deck how to make them. The waiter brought us each our last drinks at three in the morning, saying he was off for the night. We stayed talking and laughing until the sun rose.

I hadn't wanted to, but somewhere along the line during the night, I told her exactly how Bobby had died. And how I'd exacted my vengeance.

She held my hand and cried.

At first I felt stupid, but then I was relieved I'd told her.

"Then you killed that man?"

I nodded.

We sat there in silence for a while.

"I had no idea." She rubbed my fingers with hers. "And you said you are an orphan like me? You have had a lot of loss for someone our age."

"Your parents are dead?" I sat up.

"They were killed in a fire." Her voice was quiet.

I remembered her telling the captain about her fear of fire.

"I'm so sorry." For a second I'd been about to say my parents had also died in a fire, but that wasn't true. That was what the murderers had wanted me to believe. The fire had been set to try to hide the bullets in their foreheads.

"I didn't think I wanted to live anymore," she said. "But then I met Henry."

"It was recent?"

She didn't answer. With the sky lightening to a pale pink in the east, Natasha stood, wrapping the blanket around her small frame. "I'm the walking dead. I need to go to bed. We are going to have a busy day in Gibraltar. I need my beauty sleep."

8

TROUBLE IN PARADISE

The next evening, after spending the day in Gibraltar—exploring Michael's caves and swimming with the dolphins—we said our goodbyes at the pool.

As we did, a shadow passed over Natasha's gorgeous features. I followed her gaze. Henry was standing on the balcony again, but instead of smiling or raising his glass he turned and went inside.

"Everything okay?" I asked.

Natasha burst into laughter. "Yes. He just wants to get laid. I know that look. I'll have to leave in a few minutes. See you at eight for dinner."

I smiled back. My heart was full. I had a real friend. The shroud of loneliness that had been so constant I'd never even noticed it, was gone. In its place was a lightness and feeling of hope and renewal and possibility.

∼

I AIMED smiles at my dining table companions as I took my seat at dinner. I'd worn a full-length gown that Dante had made me pack. It was exquisite: a spaghetti-strapped, ankle-length, white-beaded dress that I wore with dangling diamond earrings. I felt so glamorous. It was a far cry from my leather pants and ripped T-shirt uniform back home in San Francisco. Thank God Dante was my wardrobe consultant and buyer most of the time.

Natasha and Henry hadn't arrived yet. I made polite conversation with the couple to my left. They were from Canada, so, of course, they were extraordinarily pleasant.

But I kept glancing anxiously at the staircase. Natasha had mentioned Henry's health not being the best. I hoped everything was okay. But then I remembered she'd left earlier because Henry was horny.

They were probably still in bed. Good for them.

Our waiter brought out a platter of massive scallops in butter with a flourish. It wasn't until I was halfway through the fish entrée that Natasha and Henry appeared.

Her eyes were swollen and red. Definitely not sporting a freshly-fucked look. More of a spent-the-afternoon-arguing-with-the-man-I-love-and-crying look.

Henry didn't look so hot, either. He looked weary and shot me a polite smile that didn't reach his eyes. Maybe Henry found out about Natasha's late night escapade the other night. She'd said she usually confessed to him after she strayed. But she didn't mention that he took it badly.

But, of course, he would. Even if he forgave her, he was justified in being pissed off.

While he greeted the other members of the table, I shot Natasha a questioning glance, but she shook her head nearly imperceptibly and looked away.

Dinner was tense. Natasha stabbed at her mahi-mahi with a steak knife, and the sound of the knife scraping the china grated. I noticed the woman across from me grimacing. Everybody at the table tried to ignore the awkward tension.

I couldn't help but stare at Henry. His easygoing manner had vanished. Usually, he indulged every little whim Natasha had. He didn't care if she was rude or broke outside the boundaries of societal norms. He looked benevolently on her and let her do as she would.

Now, he leaned down and scolded Natasha for something. I couldn't make out what he said, but her cheeks grew red.

I wondered if these three days together at sea were wearing on the couple. Although she doted on him, I noticed she also spent a lot of time away from him. Maybe that's what worked for them. Who was *I* to judge?

But their spat—or whatever it was—made the whole table uncomfortable. I tried to ignore them and turned to my seatmate to the left. He was a financier from Lyons, France, and the more we spoke, the sexier he became. I could definitely see the appeal of an older, powerful, successful man. He was there with his wife, an equally interesting person, who owned a skin care company that was hot with celebrities. She was in an animated discussion with the man on her other side.

Every time I glanced over at Natasha, she looked like she was about to cry. She kept her eyes down on her plate, picking at her meal. Henry would occasionally say something in her ear, and she would nod, grim-faced.

He knew about the blonde. That had to be it.

She said she always ended up confessing to him.

Maybe that other woman had said something, made a scene.

I glanced around the dining room. I saw several blond heads but couldn't tell where she was. Plus, there were two separate dinner hours. But then I spotted Sharon Long. She was staring right at me. I could feel the heat spread across my cheeks and I had no idea why. She winked at me and raised her wine glass to me in a toast. I quickly shot a glance at Natasha, but she wasn't paying attention. I looked away and then next time I glanced over at the other table, Sharon Long was in an animated conversation with the man beside her.

After dessert was served, without even glancing down at the elaborate chocolate mousse mountain placed in front of him, Henry abruptly stood and touched Natasha's elbow. "Excuse us, we are going to skip after dinner drinks and retire to our room early tonight. It's been a long day."

Natasha wouldn't meet my eyes. Guess dancing was out. She turned and followed Henry out of the room.

Soon, all my dining companions had excused themselves, and I was alone.

It wasn't long after that I was kicked out of the dining room and had my dalliance with Sal the bartender and the uptight fuck in the Star Bar. In the pre-dawn sky, I made my way to the Sun Deck and sidled up to the railing with my bourbon. Ten minutes later came the scream.

9

I DO WHAT I WANT

It was Natasha.

I don't know how I knew, but I did.

Racing to the elevator, I punched the up button. As the door slid open, two men in black uniforms with patches that said "Security" ran up and stepped through the open elevator doors.

"Ma'am, we're going to have to ask you to wait here."

"That was my friend who screamed. I'm coming, too."

Before they could protest, the elevator door slid closed.

One man held his security badge up to a sensor and then punched the buttons for the penthouse level.

When the doors skimmed open, we were in the foyer of the penthouse. Nightsticks at the ready, the men ignored me and headed further inside the space. I followed them into a living room and then heard one of them say, "Ma'am, are you okay?"

Natasha was slumped just inside the open doorway in a puddle of ivory silk. Her hands were covered in blood, and her red silken hair was over her face.

She didn't answer. One man leaned down and said in a low voice. "Are you injured?"

Shaking her head, she stared at her hands. Standing, the man jutted his chin toward the far end of the suite. The guards spread off, searching the penthouse, nightsticks at the ready.

I crouched down by Natasha and lifted her chin. "What's wrong? Are you okay?"

She shook her head.

"Are you hurt? Is this your blood?"

Again, she shook her head. I didn't see any obvious wounds on her.

"Where is Henry?"

She didn't answer, just rotated her bloody hands in front of her, staring at them. I grabbed her chin and made her gaze meet mine.

"Natasha," I said firmly. "Where is Henry?"

Finally, she answered. "I don't know."

Soon, the security guards were back and on their radios, talking low. I'd managed to help Natasha up and was sitting with her on one of the couches in the penthouse.

I had my arm around her and murmured soothing sounds in her ear.

She was in shock.

I looked over her head at one of the security guards. "Can you please call the ship doctor?"

He was younger than the other with tightly shorn brown hair, bulky muscles, and a little rash on his jaw from shaving. I clocked him in a heartbeat. Four years in the military. Didn't fit in. Probably booted out. Tried for a cop job, but nobody would have him because of his dishonorable discharge. Thought security on a cruise ship would be a kickback gig and an easy way to travel and meet women in bikinis. He never expected tonight.

He stared at me blankly for a second and then nodded. He stepped into the other room, and I heard him speaking urgently to someone on the other end of the radio.

Natasha wasn't crying, but her entire body shook in my embrace. I pulled a throw blanket over her. As we waited, I took in the penthouse for the first time. From my perch on the edge of the massive circular white couch, it looked like the suite was bigger than my entire loft by a few times over.

Nothing to sneeze at. Chandeliers. A black marble dining room table. Murano glass bowls on open shelving. A goddamn Steinway grand piano. And the painting sure as hell looked like an original DeKoonig. An entire wall of mirrors. Private balconies. Hell, I could see the water of a private pool glinting in the moonlight on the private deck.

Several doorways led to other areas.

From what I could see, the balcony stretched the entire length of one side of the penthouse.

Natasha hadn't moved. I crouched in front of her.

"What's going on? Where is Henry, Natasha?"

She met my eyes and sadly shook her head.

"Is this his blood?" I took her wrists. I stood, looking for a sink.

"Please stay where you are until the detective arrives." It was the security guard. "She asked that everything remain untouched."

I nodded and crouched back down by Natasha.

In a low voice, I said, "The detective is going to be here in a second and is going to ask you what happened. Why don't you practice and tell me?"

She closed her eyes for a second and then nodded.

Henry had been angry at her all day because the other night she'd brought that blonde woman back to the suite.

"You brought her back here?" I asked, incredulous.

"I should've just brought her to bed with him, then it would've been fine, but I didn't want to share." She stared straight ahead as she spoke, rubbing her bloody hands on her silky nightgown, leaving rust stains and streaks. "I took her to one of the other bedrooms."

Then she asked for money. She said if I didn't give her fifty thousand dollars she'd tell Henry."

Natasha swiveled her head and looked at me. She waited as if I was supposed to say something, so I said, "Did you?"

"No. That's ridiculous. I wasn't going to give her any money. She could tell Henry anything she wanted. I do what I want. He lets me do whatever I want."

"So what's the problem?"

"I thought it was over. I told her I would tell Henry myself, and there was nothing she could do to hurt us. But then she came here before dinner." Natasha looked down. "I didn't know it, but she took a video. Her phone was recording us the whole time. And she said she was going to send them to the tabloids, the paparazzi."

I stood and poured us both drinks, even though the detective has asked us not to touch anything. I gulped mine, refilled it, and then handed Natasha hers. She held it in trembling hands, dipping her head to take a small sip before continuing.

"So before dinner I told him about us. He was angry. It wasn't until after dinner while we were in the hot tub, that Henry said he wanted me to move out of our suite for the rest of the cruise. I was heartbroken. So, I left. I didn't know where to go so I went to see her. And now he's dead."

The blonde.

It stung that she would go to that stranger, a blackmailing stranger, instead of me—her friend, but I let it go.

"Shhhh," I said, rubbing her arm. "You said you don't know that he's dead. He's missing right now. We don't know anything."

"Look," she held out her hands. They were caked in blood. She was right. The blood told a different story.

"When did you see him last?"

"I left Greta's cabin about three. I figured Henry would be asleep and I could just sneak in and try to get him to forgive me when he woke."

Back in the penthouse, she showered and then slipped into bed, but Henry was not there. She assumed he was angry and sleeping in a spare bedroom. But later in the night, a noise startled her awake, and she called out for him.

He didn't answer, so she got up to find him.

The first places she looked were the other two bedrooms, but they were empty. So were all the other rooms in the penthouse. Heart pounding, she even checked the hot tub, terror streaking through her at the thought that maybe he'd had a heart attack in the tub after she'd left. But the hot tub was empty and the jets were off. That's when she saw the open doors to the massive deck surrounding the penthouse. As soon as she stepped outside, she saw something wet on the deck and smeared on the rail. She reached down and touched it before realizing it was blood, she said.

And that's when she screamed.

"It's okay. It could have been someone else's blood," I said, patting her skinny knee through the silk fabric. But we both knew I was lying. It was Henry's blood.

"Oh my God. What will I do without him?"

At those words, I looked up and saw a woman standing there staring at us, eyes narrowed. She was tall and wore her brown hair pulled back in a severe bun. She wore khaki pants, a coral top and brown loafers. Her gaze was cold and calculating.

"Who are you?" I said.

"I'm Detective Solange."

Right then, I knew Natasha was a suspect. I leaned over and whispered in her ear. "Do you want a lawyer?"

Natasha drew back in horror and flung my hand away. "What? What are you talking about? No! No! What are you saying?"

I closed my eyes for a second. "Sorry. I know you didn't do anything," I said in a low voice. But I didn't like the look in that woman's eyes.

"Thank you for sitting with Mrs. Ainsley until I could get here. We will no longer need your help."

I blinked. But I didn't budge.

"Please excuse us now." She was a persistent little copper, wasn't she?

"I'll leave if Natasha wants me to leave." I said, meeting her eyes.

Natasha burst into tears. "Just go, Gia. Just go."

"Are you sure?"

She sniffled and swiped at her eyes. "Yes."

"Fine. I'll be in my suite if you need me."

She didn't answer. I cast one look back before I walked out. The detective had taken my spot on the couch and was leaning, speaking to Natasha. My new friend nodded once and looked back at me with terrified, wide eyes.

10

POKER HAND

Natasha didn't answer my calls throughout the night, so in the morning, feeling adrift and worried about her, I pulled on my red crocheted bikini, grabbed a flask full of bourbon and my beach towel and headed for the pool. I was hoping she would show up at our usual meeting place. Or, if she went out on her balcony, she could see me there. I sent her a text saying, "At pool. Call me when you get up."

Spreading my towel out, I plopped on my stomach, took a big gulp of my whisky and put my head down, staring up at the window from the privacy of my sunglasses. No movement. Also, with my gaze hidden behind dark sunglasses, I examined every blonde that walked across the deck to the café that served lunch. I figured the pool deck outside the café would be the most likely place to spot the blonde. *Greta.* Unless, of course, she ordered room service. Or just didn't eat.

I waited until about three, but with the warmth of the sun on me like a drug, I could no longer fight the heaviness in my limbs and drifted off to sleep.

When I woke, I sat up and stretched. The sun was dipping on the horizon. I checked my phone. Nothing. Damn.

A waiter headed my way. "May I bring you something?"

My stomach grumbled a little at the words. "Yes, please."

Before I could order, he turned and walked away. Okay. Whatever.

I leaned back and closed my eyes.

A few minutes later, the waiter reappeared with a tray of cheese, crackers, grapes, tiny toasts with caviar, a bottle of white wine, and a small dish of shrimp, scallops, and crab bathed in butter with a hunk of bread to dip into the buttery broth.

"Wow," I said and sat up straight. "Thank you. I'm in room—"

"It is already taken care of," he said.

I scrunched my face. He raised his eyes. I looked over and saw Natasha standing on the balcony. She still wore the ivory silk nightgown she'd worn the night before. It blew in the breeze, along with her hair. She stood for a moment looking down at me and then turned and went inside.

After I polished off lunch and the bottle of wine, I tugged a black sundress over my swimsuit and headed for the bank of elevators that led to the penthouses.

Of course, once the elevator opened and I stepped inside, I realized I was going nowhere.

I didn't have the code for the keypad and didn't have the keycard to swipe.

I grabbed my phone and texted Natasha. "Help. stuck in your elevator. come get me."

A minute later this text appeared: "#0407#. They let us program our own code. How cool is that?"

I punched the number into the keypad. Boom.

The elevator whooshed up, and the doors opened into a small foyer.

I didn't see her anywhere. "Hey?"

Nothing.

Then I saw her. She was standing on the big balcony with her back to me, looking out over the sea. When I reached her side, she didn't turn. She just kept staring sightlessly at the sea churning in the boat's wake below. Her hands clenched the railing so tightly her knuckles were white. The rail was wet from the tears dripping off her cheeks.

"What can I do?" I said in a soft voice.

She turned. "I don't know."

"What does that detective say?"

"They are treating *me* like a suspect. Me!" Her eyes were wild. "How dare they?"

"That's crazy," I said.

She sniffled and nodded.

"I told them she did it, but they still are treating me like a suspect."

I froze. "Who is *she*?"

Natasha looked at me with wide eyes. "Sharon Long."

"I don't understand."

"She couldn't have him so nobody could. She killed him. I know it," Natasha said. She reached into my bag and plucked out my cigarettes, lighting one. "I even showed that detective the note."

Sharon Long had written Henry a note saying she'd rather see him dead than with Natasha.

"That's pretty incriminating," I said.

"Right?" Natasha blew a perfect smoke ring. "And she doesn't have an alibi for last night."

"Holy shit."

"But they still are treating me like a suspect. They said they aren't sure I should get off the ship in Tangier."

"That's crazy. You're not under arrest. They can't keep you." I said it, but I wasn't sure. Maybe ships had different rules.

I remembered that the detective had first suspected me in Bobby's murder and how furious and helpless I had felt. I knew how awful it was to be in a deep pit of hopeless grief while also being treated as a suspect. I also remembered how it felt to have just lost the man I loved. There was only one thing that had kept me going. And that's when I knew what I could do. I leaned forward.

"When they murdered Bobby, I couldn't rest, couldn't sleep, couldn't think, until I found out who did it." *And killed them.*

She nodded but seemed unconvinced.

"If Sharon Long did this, maybe we can find some way to prove it," I said.

"Maybe she paid someone. I don't think a woman would be capable of overpowering Henry. I mean, he was a big man," Natasha said. "But I know she's behind it somehow."

"You think there's any chance he's alive somewhere? Maybe on board hurt or something?"

Natasha gasped and threw her palm to her mouth and walked inside, plopping on the couch. "Oh my God, I never thought of that!"

Then she frowned. "But the blood."

"Yeah." The blood. "Any chance he injured himself, went to get patched up, and didn't come back?"

"No. He's dead," she said with a sob. "Someone hurt him and threw him overboard. I just know it. And the detectives are asking me questions. So many questions."

"Don't worry. We'll figure out who did this, and the detective will leave you be."

She nodded and leaned her head back against the couch cushion.

"Have you slept?"

"I tried. The ship doctor gave me those." She gestured toward a small prescription bottle. I picked it up. It didn't have a label.

"What are they?"

"A sedative or sleeping pill," she said. "I didn't want to take them. I was afraid whoever hurt Henry would come back for me."

"I can stay here while you nap." I grabbed a bottle of sparkling water off the bar, plucked a pill out of the container, and handed everything to her. "Here, you need to sleep."

Natasha turned toward me. "Will you stay with me? Will you stay with me? You can stay in one of the spare bedrooms? I'm too afraid to sleep here alone."

I hesitated for a second. But a good friend would say yes, so I nodded.

Her shoulders slumped in relief.

She took the pill from me and swallowed. Before long, she curled her legs up on the couch under her and closed her eyes. Soon, she was emitting soft snoring sounds.

I went to find the bathroom. The first door I came to led to the master suite, and I saw the open door to a bathroom beyond it. After using the bathroom, I lingered in the bedroom.

It was so sweet, they'd brought a photo of themselves and propped it on a dresser across from the bed among assorted bits of jewelry, makeup, and perfume. It looked like they'd been living there for years. I picked up the photo.

Natasha was glowing. Her face was tilted, looking up at Henry with love.

Henry looked down on her with a dimpled smile. He was pretty cute for an old guy. A stab of grief took my breath away. He was probably dead. I bit my lip. I wasn't going to cry. Christ, I'd barely known the guy. But I'd find whoever had killed him and make them pay.

I put the picture down and tugged open the top drawer of the dresser. I was hoping to find something comfortable for Natasha to wear to get her out of the bloodstained one.

The top drawer was empty. And the next one. And so on.

I looked around. The walk-in closet. Of course. She probably even hung up her silk nighties. I tugged a pair of yoga pants and a cozy-looking sweatshirt off a hanger. When I did, I noticed a small silver case tucked back under the hanging clothes

Something she'd said earlier had been nagging at me. I'd let it go at the time, but now it came back as I stood in her closet.

She was afraid they'd come back and search her suite. Of course, to me that offhanded comment meant that the couple had something to hide. But what?

A jewelry box full of illegal diamonds? Drugs? Paperwork of illegal financial transactions?

Maybe it was in the silver case she'd tucked behind all her clothes.

I pulled it out. It had a combination lock. I tried the code for the elevator she'd given me earlier. It worked.

At first I wasn't sure what I was looking at. A stack of passports.

Picking them up, I rifled through them like a poker hand. Five in all. A sound in the living room made me freeze. Then I heard it again—it sounded like she was moaning in her sleep. When I didn't hear anything again for a few seconds, I quickly flipped through them. All Natasha's gorgeous face with different names. Nadine Romanoff. Laura Matthers. Nancy Shostakova. Czarina Karliff. Yelena Belova. Jesus. It didn't make any sense. Was she and Henry who they claimed? Maybe Henry was up to something nefarious, something illegal that had caused his death.

From the living room, I heard Natasha again. This time calling my name. With trembling hands, I shoved the passports back in the case, snapped it closed, and shoved it back where I found it.

Scooping up the clothes, I hurried into the living room.

"I found these. You should change out of that nightgown."

Looking down at the nightgown, she nodded but slumped back onto the couch, eyes half slit.

"I'm too tired."

"You can wait until morning if you want, but you need to shower and change, okay?"

"I woke up and you weren't here," she said in a plaintive voice. "Where were you?"

"Getting you clean clothes. I told you."

"Oh yeah." She started to fall asleep again then jerked and opened her eyes. "Gia? Gia?"

Her voice was frantic.

"I'm here, Natasha." I reached over and squeezed her hand.

She clutched it like a lifeline. "Please stay here with me. I'm afraid. I don't want to be alone. Please?"

"Sure. Of course." I let go of her hand and settled back on the couch. "I'll be right here. Just sleep now."

As soon as her eyes closed, my shoulders slumped in relief. This mothering, nurturing, caretaking stuff was fucking exhausting. I wasn't cut out for it. It took all my effort to stay and console her when a small, irritated part of me wanted to take off and go back to my own bed.

Part of it was that it was disconcerting to see a strong woman reduced to needy mush. But hell, her husband was gone, probably murdered. And the detectives were treating her like a suspect. I knew how that felt. Shitty. I'd try to be more compassionate. That's what friends did. I had a lot to learn.

Within a few seconds, I heard the soft sounds of her sleeping. Her eyelids fluttered slightly. I glanced over at the door to the bedroom and closet but then dimmed the light on the table between us and lay back, closing my eyes.

Maybe I'd ask her about the passports in the morning. Or maybe I'd find out what was going on by myself.

11

CASABLANCA

When I woke in the morning, Natasha was in the shower. I figured that was a good sign.

Stretching, I glanced out the window to see sunshine reflecting off a bright blue sea. I padded into the kitchen to forage for coffee beans.

By the time the coffee had percolated, Natasha came out dressed in ivory slacks and a pale pink silky tank top with her wet hair pulled back into a ponytail.

"How do you feel?"

"Fuzzy. I don't like sleeping pills." She slumped on the bar stool across from me.

I handed her a cup of coffee and took her in.

"Well you look a lot better. You needed sleep."

"I'm never going to care about how I look again."

"That's silly," I said.

We sat there in silence for a moment sipping our coffee. Then the boat engines, a constant rumble and vibration, turned off. We both glanced toward the wall of windows.

"Oh!" Her exclamation was the first time I'd heard any energy in her voice since she'd found Henry missing.

The endless blue of the sea had been replaced with square white buildings perched on a hillside reflected the sunrise. Small oats dotted the water between the cruise ship and shore. Tangier. Morocco.

We both went out on the balcony. I lit two cigarettes and handed her one.

"It's just like I imagined it," Natasha said in a small voice. "I'd told Henry I'd always dreamed of coming here. Casablanca is my very favorite movie of all time. I watched it when I was fifteen, and it changed my life. I had no idea life could be like that. That's one reason he booked this trip." She turned to me. "This vacation was partly so I could go to Casablanca. Henry didn't care where we went. He just wanted me to be happy. You see, I didn't grow up rich like Henry."

I tried to not act surprised.

"I grew up poor in the Ukraine. In fact," she cast a glance my way. "I grew up with a different name. Natalie. I invented Natasha as soon as I left our village at eighteen. I never want to be Natalie again. She is homely and shy and awkward. But Natasha is chic and flirtatious and confident."

All I could think about was the stack of passports. "Did you legally change your name?"

"Huh?" She shot me a quick glance.

"Are you still legally Natalie?" I held my breath waiting.

"No. I changed my name to Natasha when I married Henry. When you fill out the marriage license, you can become anyone you want."

"You said you left your home when you were eighteen, but you've only been married to Henry for six months. When exactly did you become Natasha?"

"Why are you asking me all these questions?" She turned and walked back inside.

I went inside when I heard the elevator ding. I hovered in the background, pretending to snoop in the refrigerator for breakfast as Natasha headed to the foyer.

I recognized the voice right away.

Detective Solange.

"This is our first port of call since your husband disappeared. We are keeping track of who gets on and off the ship. Trust me, we will know if someone gets off and doesn't return. But we have you signed up for the day trip to Casablanca. I wanted to know if you are planning on going?"

"No. God no," Natasha said.

"Good," the detective said.

I stepped into the room. I watched the detective carefully, but she didn't act surprised to see me there.

"Of course, she's going," I said. I turned toward Natasha. "You told me earlier you'd dreamed of coming here ever since you were a child. You are going."

"But that was before," she said.

"I think it's a good idea." I said, crossing my arms.

Detective Solange remained expressionless. I turned to her.

"Unless she's under arrest, I see no reason she can't take the excursion to shore."

The seconds stretched in silence, and finally the detective nodded slowly.

"You said you are keeping track of who comes and goes off the ship, right?" I said. "What about Sharon Long? You are keeping track of her whereabouts I hope?"

The detective raised an eyebrow.

"We have this under control, thank you for your concern." She punched the elevator button. "I will keep you apprised of the investigation. We will have more experts on the case once we reach Lisbon."

After the elevator doors slid closed, I stubbed out my cigarette.

"I need to go back to my cabin to change and shower. Are you going to be okay here in the meantime?"

She smiled and nodded. "Yes. I think so. I'm just worried about being alone when I sleep or shower. I should be fine now. Can I meet you at your cabin in an hour?"

I gave her the suite number and headed back. After a long

shower, I took my time doing my makeup, sipping on a small glass of bourbon.

When she arrived, Natasha actually looked a little bit back to normal.

She wore a snug white tank top, a flowing pink and orange print maxi skirt, and tan gladiator sandals. An oversize, filmy pink wrap was draped across her shoulders, and she wore massive white-framed sunglasses. As soon as she came in, she pushed up her sunglasses, flung her wrap on my bed and looked around with wide eyes.

"This is nice."

"Very funny."

She cracked a grin. It was a hovel compared to her penthouse.

"Gia, don't forget I didn't grow up rich. I'm not spoiled."

"That's true." I smiled. "It's probably why we get along so well."

She threw open my closet doors. "I couldn't decide what to wear. Can I see what you have?"

I swallowed my irritation. Maybe this is what female friends did. Snooped. Then I was flushed with guilt. I'd sure as hell snooped in her closet, hadn't I?

"Uh, sure. Go ahead and look." I eyed her long skirt. It probably wasn't the best choice. I could imagine it sweeping up all the dirt as we walked city streets and temples.

Leaning over my dresser mirror, I finished applying dark kohl around my eyes. I'd pulled on some black linen ankle pants and a black linen button down top, leaving the top button undone. Worn with espadrilles, a large straw hat, and dark sunglasses, I was ready to explore Morocco.

"This! This is cute!" She pulled out a strapless red sundress. "Can I try it on?"

"It's probably not great for sightseeing. Aren't we visiting caves and mausoleums?"

She frowned. "Yeah, you're right."

My fingers itched to grab her arm and yank her away from my things. But I'd done even worse with my own snooping. I wondered if

Henry had a stack of fake IDs as well. Maybe they were con artists, maybe that's why he'd been killed. My eyes widened at the thought.

"Hey, why did you change your name again?"

She froze.

Well, it was awkward. There was no reason for my question. No context. Nothing.

I watched her back stiffen. I couldn't see her face. Then she exclaimed loudly. "These! Please can I try them on? Like you said, I'll be doing touristy things. This skirt isn't very practical."

She held out a pair of white Capri pants.

I shrugged. White was still a shitty choice but possibly a tad better than that long-ass skirt she had on. "I'm not sure we're the same size, but go for it." I watched her. It hadn't escaped me that she'd deftly avoided my question about changing her name.

"I'll just go in the bathroom and try them on where there is a good mirror," she said. Leaning over she plucked her bag from the top of my dresser. "Besides I have to fix my makeup."

I was surprised by her modesty. But whatever.

Like I kept being reminded: I didn't know how to do girlfriends. I'd only had boyfriends.

After a few minutes, she came out in the pants. They fit perfectly.

"Do you mind? I love them."

"Wear them. It's fine." I tried to smile, even though I was slightly annoyed. God, this girly stuff was exhausting. I glanced at my watch. "We've got to go."

I followed her out, but as soon as we were in the hall, she slapped her palm to her head. "Oh, shoot. I left my lipstick in your bathroom. Do you mind?" She gestured to the door.

If she said, "Do you mind?" one more time I was going to scream. Guys didn't say that. Why did women? I wasn't sure if I said it, too, but I vowed to never say it again.

I punched in my code.

"I'll be right back," she said and slipped inside.

I leaned against the wall in the hall. It was nice to see Natasha back to normal but it was tiring to be around her. Did all female friends need this much attention and energy? Guys were so much easier. They said what they thought and didn't preface everything by making sure the other person was okay with what they said and did.

Men suited me much better.

But I couldn't help but smile. I liked being friends with Natasha. It was fun. Fun wasn't necessarily a natural part of my life. It was something that had definitely been missing. But then I remembered the stack of passports. What was that about? I didn't think I should trust Natasha. Not just yet. She was hiding something. And what the hell was taking her so long? I moved to the door, ready to punch the keypad, when it opened.

"Sorry," she said and looped her arm through mine. "You ready? I'm so excited!" But then her smile faded. "God, I'm a beast. I feel so guilty. Henry is dead and here I am acting giddy about going to Casablanca."

I also felt torn. As if we should be tracking down and confronting Sharon Long instead of gallivanting around in Africa. But I also knew Natasha needed to do this. It was a small thing that would help take her mind off her grief.

"Natasha," I said. "It's okay. Really. I've been where you are. You still have to live. It's okay to find joy even as you grieve. When someone you love dies, it doesn't mean you have to die with them."

Shaking her head, she kept walking without answering.

12

CHOP-CHOP

Tangier

The sun beat down on us without mercy.

We savored our view of Morocco from the harbor as our ship coasted in to the dock.

White-washed buildings—Andalusian, Moorish, and Colonial styles—dotted the hillside before us.

As soon as we stepped onto land, we were assaulted with the smoky, spicy smells of Morocco. It smelled warm and fragrant like a sultry exotic perfume. I inhaled deeply and stretched.

To my right, a golden beach was dotted with figures in colorful swimsuits and, to my surprise, camels! I spotted three of them on the beach before I was shuttled off to a van waiting to take us into Tangier proper.

Even though it was less than one hundred feet from the port turnstile to our waiting driver, no fewer than three men approached and offered to give us private tours of the city.

Natasha kept her head high and averted her eyes, as if she were a celebrity fending off paparazzi. I wasn't so passive.

When one man reached for Natasha, saying he'd pay twenty

camels for a redhead like her, I grasped his wrist and twisted it so hard he howled in pain. He scowled and took off as soon as I released him. I raised my eyebrow at his companion, who glared at me but then slunk off to accost some Canadian tourists.

Mosquitos. I remembered hearing someone on the ship saying the hawkers who greet the cruise ship tourists were called this. That's fine. I had no problem squishing pesky bugs. Especially if they bit.

But we weren't staying in Tangier long. We had a hot date with Casablanca. We'd have time to explore the medina and do some shopping later. We were the only ones on our small cruise ship that had opted for the Casablanca leg of the excursion, so we got a private tour vehicle—a new SUV.

Our driver waited at the appointed meeting place and introduced himself as Chop-Chop.

"As in C-H-O-P C-H-O-P?" I asked.

He nodded with a big grin.

"Okay," I said, and got in.

We stopped at the Cave of Hercules where the sea pours in through an opening that is the shape of Africa and then traveled along the coast with stunning views of the ocean.

As we approached the legendary city, Casablanca didn't look to be anything special. A big metro area with skyscrapers.

Natasha's face fell.

"This is it?" Her voice was soft.

"I had no idea it was a big city," I said.

Chop-Chop shrugged. "It's modern. This is industrial center of Morocco. The port is one of the largest artificial ports in the world."

"It's just so...big," Natasha said.

"Nearly 4 million in city. About 7 million in area," he said.

But once we got out of our vehicle, Natasha was like a little girl. Curious about everything and exclaiming over the architecture, the people, the bazaar—called a souk—and the Hassan II Mosque. There was still a heavy pallor of sadness over her, though.

I'd catch her with a look of sorrow wiping away a stray tear, but then turning to me to try to smile. I didn't know what to do or say except be there for her.

We stopped for Moroccan mint tea and tiny pastries for a late lunch before we got back in the SUV for the Casablanca movie portion of the tour. It essentially consisted of a visit to Rick's Café in the old medina section of the city. But it was a replica of the nightclub used in the movie. As soon as we pulled up and Natasha saw the masses of white tourists wearing spandex and fanny packs, her mood grew sour.

"I don't want to go inside," she said. "It will ruin the image I have in my mind. It is a tourist trap."

She was right.

"Should we go somewhere else?" I asked.

She nodded furiously.

"I hate it. I hate that they did that." Her voice was vicious. I'd never heard her angry so this surprised me. "A fake. They ruined everything."

Her phone buzzed and she glanced down at it and scowled.

"What is it?"

"Oh, nothing. The detective asking when we were coming back aboard?"

"Really?" It was my turn to scowl.

"It's fine," she said.

"They're grasping at straws. She's a rent-a-cop. Not a real detective anyway. As soon as we get to Lisbon, they'll bring the big guns aboard."

She frowned. "Why Lisbon?"

"I think because Henry is a EU citizen they want it investigated that way."

Nodding, she leaned forward and spoke in Chop-Chop's ear. "Can we go back to Tangier early?"

He nodded. She sat back and closed her eyes.

For a second I was going to argue with her and say maybe I wasn't done with Casablanca. But I was. It was her dream. Not mine.

The sun was low in the sky when we arrived back in Tangier and Chop-Chop dropped us off at what he called "a hidden treasure" restaurant.

It was at the far edge of the medina—the old walled city within Tangier. The medina was comprised of a labyrinth of narrow, winding streets for pedestrians only and was surrounded by the walls of a 15th century fortress.

We sat at an outside table and took in the scenery. The sidewalk café gave us ample opportunities for people watching. Down the street, boys kicked around a soccer ball. Men wearing *djellabas* clustered in corners, smoking. Women carrying baskets laden with vegetables passed by. A few Americans and Europeans wandered past, clutching plastic bags of souvenirs.

I kept an eye out in case Sharon Long passed by. I wasn't yet convinced she'd murdered Henry, but I sure as hell had a few things to ask her about. So far, she looked good for it.

A waiter brought us fragrant bowls of tagine and thick bread to sop it up with, some couscous with herbs and more mint tea. Natasha ordered a bottle of wine, and I didn't object.

We didn't have to return to the ship until seven.

Natasha kept glancing at her phone.

I was getting antsy. The sightseeing was fun, but I was eager to confront Sharon Long.

"Do you think she stayed onboard the ship?" I asked.

Natasha knew who I was talking about.

"I have no idea. Hopefully, they've arrested her by now."

"Are you still getting texts from Solange?"

She didn't answer.

After our meal, I downed the rest of my wine and stood, eager to start back to the ship so I could start digging around.

But Natasha grabbed my arm. "First let's have a cigarette, and then we'll go shopping."

I glanced at my watch. We still had more than an hour until the boat left for the ship. I was happy to see her good spirits restored. I sat back down and handed her my cigarette pack with my small pink lighter stuck in the plastic lining.

After we each smoked a cigarette, we headed for the heart of the medina, which lured us with exotic colors, sounds, and smells from the souk—the marketplace. Stands crowded the sides of the narrow street, filled with spices, rugs, silks, and flowers. On some stretches, women had fresh produce displayed for sale on colorful blankets.

At one stand, manned by a cute, dark-skinned vendor with a short beard and piercing blue eyes, Natasha grabbed a long, silk scarf from a table and swished it around, moving her hips suggestively to the music of a nearby lutist.

I hadn't seen those moves on the ship's dance floor.

"Brava!" I said when she was done, and both men broke into applause.

She tried to give the man money for the scarf, but he refused.

"No. You give me such pleasure knowing you will own that scarf. Please take." He put his hands together in a prayer-like gesture. "My gift." He folded it in a neat bundle and tied it with a silk ribbon.

She bowed and accepted it. We walked on.

"That was something else," I said.

As we walked through the narrow streets, she spoke without looking at me.

"Even though I grew up poor, my uncle—well, that's what we called him—paid for my Hopak dance training. It incorporates dancing, singing, martial arts, playing a musical instrument, sword fighting, and becoming fluent in several languages."

I thought about what she said. "Sounds like finishing school for bad ass girls to me. Sign me up."

She looked down. "It is only for men. My uncle chopped off my hair and made me dress like a man for the training."

"He made you pretend to be a boy?"

Her voice grew low, and she turned away, but before she did, I saw that her eyes were bright with either sadness or anger, I couldn't tell. "Among other things."

I touched her arm. "I'm so sorry."

She shrugged. "I'm happy now that I have the training."

Natasha wandered off a bit ahead of me, saying something about finding a pink Turkish towel. I let her have her space and turned to buy an exquisite, blue glass jar of saffron.

By the time the man had given me my change, Natasha was nowhere to be found.

13

HURTS LIKE A MOTHERFUCKER

The rows of vendors were crowded with people huddling on each side, their dark heads pressed close together. No redhead, though.

I quickly made my way through the crowd, jostling people and standing on tiptoe to see. Natasha was gone. I was near the end of the row of stands when I saw a flash of red hair about half a block down the street.

"Natasha!" I yelled. A few people cast annoyed glances at me, but I didn't care. I took off at a sprint toward the other end of the street in time to see a glimpse of a redheaded woman dipping into an alley.

By the time I made it to the entrance and peered down it, I couldn't see a thing. It was a long, narrow, twisting, dark path. "Natasha?" My voice echoed. I stepped into the passage and realized that there were several small passageways that spoked off from the main alley. She could be anywhere. I reached for my phone. No service. Of course.

Wishing I had my gun, I made my way down into the dark alley, hands in front of me, ready to fight if I needed to. What the hell was Natasha doing taking off like that?

I peered down first passageway. A square of light spilled out of an open door with delicious smells. A man stepped out, threw something into a trashcan and lit a cigarette. I kept walking. The second passageway, on the opposite side of the alley was less welcoming. I squinted but couldn't make out much beyond a few dark shapes. An eerie scratching noise filtered out of the blackness.

The scratching was replaced by a scrabbling and then silence. I waited. And then in the silence, I heard a sound. A sigh. What sounded like a woman's mournful sigh. A familiar sigh. Casting one last glance behind me at the lights and sounds of the medina, I stepped into the passageway, holding my breath, straining to see and hear.

Halfway down the passage, my eyes adjusted, and I saw that one of the many doorways was wide open. I peered inside cautiously. The inside was dimly lit. It was a long room, but at the other end I saw another flash of red disappear through a doorway.

This time I raced inside, flinging caution aside. I wasn't sure what Natasha was up to, but I was tired of the cat and mouse game. I ran through the room, dodging dark shapes of furniture and plowed through the doorway where she'd gone.

It opened into a small kitchen and then on the other side, an open door leading back outside to another alley. Shit.

I poked my head out, looking both ways and was about to step outside when an excruciating pain exploded in my head. I crumpled. On my knees, I reached behind me to protect myself from another attack. All sounds were blotted out by a long, horrifying scream. I gave in to gravity and curled up into a ball, clutching my head, trying to stop the pain. And then all was black.

When I woke, my head throbbed and it hurt to open my eyes. I squinted and saw Natasha above me.

"Gia!" she said. "Are you okay?"

"What happened? I was following you."

"It was Sharon Long."

"What was?"

"I was following her. She was trying to flee, so I chased her. She hit you."

"She did this?" I asked.

"Yes."

"Did you see her do this?"

I blinked, trying to remember what happened before I was hit in the head, but nothing came back to me.

"We need to get you help," she said.

I closed my eyes. I heard voices and footsteps. Natasha spoke to someone in French.

The next thing I knew someone had put a pillow under my head. A few minutes later, I was on a primitive-type stretcher. I bounced atop the fabric supporting me as I was carried through the teeming streets of the medina. Bright colors, blurred faces, and whiffs of fleeting scents zipped past. Natasha's voice was close, reassuring me. "It's okay, Gia. We're bringing you back to the ship. We're getting you help. You'll be fine."

LATER, after they'd checked me out in the ship's infirmary and brought me to Natasha's spare bedroom, I kept replaying what happened. I'd stepped into an empty room, was distracted by an open door, then blasted in the head. Natasha screamed, apparently scaring my attacker, Sharon Long, off. But what happened after that?

I had a lot of questions and few answers.

And Natasha was nowhere to be found.

Finally, she appeared with the ship doctor who stuck out her hand for me to shake.

"I'm Dr. Mikki Ashe." Her hair was neat and short, and she had sparkling eyes behind silver-rimmed glasses.

"Nice to meet you," I said.

"How's the head?" she asked.

"Hurts like a motherfucker, Doc."

She chuckled. I liked her.

"I'm going to leave you with some pretty heavy duty painkillers.

They will probably make you drowsy, but that's fine. You need sleep. To rest awhile. You received a nasty blow to the head."

Natasha stood behind her, looking worried. I was worried.

I frowned. "What's a while?"

She pressed her lips together tightly. "Hard to say. But most people are fine after a day or two of rest. I'll stop back tomorrow to check on her."

"I'll stay and care for her," Natasha said. "That's why I had her brought to my suite."

The doctor turned to me. "You're lucky to have a friend like this. Your job is to rest today. When you're feeling up to it after a day or two, my prescription would be to relax by the pool."

I took in everything she said. I didn't like any of it.

But I liked her. I smiled. "Yes, ma'am." I did a half-assed salute.

She placed a prescription bottle on the nightstand beside me.

"We gave you a shot in the infirmary to ease the pain, but it's probably time to take a pill. If you stay on top of the painkillers, you will avoid a lot of unnecessary discomfort."

Natasha was immediately at my side. She tapped out a pill and handed them to me with a glass of water.

"I'm at extension thirty-two," the doctor said. "Call if you need anything or if you start to feel worse. But I think with a few days rest you're going to be just fine, Miss Santella."

I swallowed the water and pills. "Thank you so much."

Natasha walked the doctor to the door. By the time the door clicked closed, my eyes were heavy. I gave in and fell into the darkness of sleep.

In the night, I felt a hand on my shoulder. Natasha.

"Gia, it's time for your medicine."

I lifted my head and gratefully took the pills Natasha offered to me and gulped down the water in the glass she held to my lips.

In no time, I was out again.

With the light of the morning sunrise came a splitting headache. I wasn't sure what time Natasha had given me the pills in the night, but based on my pain, I was certain I was due for another dose. But they made me feel so out of it. Even as I thought this, my eyelids grew heavy and I drifted off to sleep again.

When I came to, Natasha was cradling my head, lifting it for me to take more pills.

I tried to fight her off, but I was weak. My arms seemed useless. My head throbbed.

Something I couldn't quite grasp teased at the edge of my memory. Something dangerous. "No," I finally got the word out.

"Shhh, Gia. Swallow. This will help."

I didn't want to, but didn't have the energy to resist. All I wanted to do was lie back down and close my eyes. She slipped the pills between my lips and then held the glass to my mouth. It was easier to give in. Besides, my thinking was fuzzy. Why didn't I want the medicine again?

I relented and Natasha let my head fall to the pillow.

After a few short moments, blissful blackness drifted over me like a warm, comforting blanket.

When I woke later, I was alone. In the dark.

The room twisted and writhed, and my stomach protested with an empty lurch. I closed my eyes until the vertigo subsided. My head pounded and pulsed like a jackhammer, worse than any migraine. I knew I was extraordinarily sick.

The pills.

It took a supreme amount of effort to turn my head and lift it a little. In the light streaming in from the hall I could see the pill bottle on the nightstand. I swung my arm in that direction, even though it felt like it weighed a million pounds.

As my fingers opened and closed, I realized the bottle was out of reach.

However, my hand grazed the phone. I grasped the receiver and brought it to my ear. Silence. The cord easily threaded through my hands. The phone had been disconnected.

I didn't know where my cell phone was. Or my bag.

There was something terribly wrong with me. I didn't know what it was, but I did know it had to do with Natasha. And those pills.

Just then I heard her in the other room talking to herself. I couldn't make out what she was saying, but she was angry.

I quickly pushed the phone cord back onto the nightstand and leaned my head back, closing my eyes and listening. I heard the thud of her feet hitting the ground and the padding of her footsteps. I pretended to still be asleep.

"Thank God," she said in a low whisper. Then in a louder voice she called my name.

I mumbled and shifted my head a little.

She flicked on the overhead light.

"Gia?" she repeated. "It's time for your medicine."

I blinked, fluttering my eyes.

"Do you want your medicine?"

I nodded and closed my eyes again.

She fumbled with the bottle on the nightstand. I held my breath, waiting to see if she'd notice that the phone had been moved.

"Open your mouth."

I did obediently. But this time when she put the pills in my mouth, I surreptitiously slipped them under my tongue. She didn't seem to notice, I heard her pouring water in a glass.

"Okay. Here's the water to wash them down." She placed her palm beneath my neck and lifted my head.

I opened my mouth eagerly and swallowed, keeping the pills firmly under my tongue.

Letting go of all muscle control, I let my head tilt to the side and began breathing heavily as if I'd fallen asleep.

"Gia?"

I waited in silence.

"Gia?"

I maintained my slow, steady breathing.

Then with a whoosh of air, she was gone.

I waited until I heard her in the kitchen before I slipped the pills out from under my tongue and hid them under my pillow. I managed to get myself propped up on one arm and stretched my fingers toward the small, brown bottle. I fumbled with the cap, trying to keep the pills inside from rattling around and giving me away. After what seemed like an eternity, the cap fell onto the sheets beside me, and I peered into the bottle. The pills were round and bright blue. I pushed the cap back onto the bottle and put it back on the table.

I reached for the phone on the nightstand. But when I held the receiver to my ear, there was no sound and I remembered it was disconnected. I set the receiver down and closed my eyes. The effort had exhausted me for some reason. And soon I was asleep again.

14

WE HAVE A PROBLEM

The sound of voices woke me later.

"She seems fine. Just sleepy." Natasha. "Doctor Ashe said she shouldn't be disturbed. I think she's planning to check in on her tomorrow."

I heard a gruff, lower voice—on the edge of a rumble. The voice was faint, but I recognized it as belonging to the detective. I tried to sit up and scream for help, but when I lifted my head, the room jerked and spun wildly again, leaving me dizzy. My voice came out as nothing more than a scratchy creak.

The voices grew quieter and then were gone entirely.

After a few seconds, I heard Natasha's panicked voice from the other room. "Fuck. Fuck. What am I going to do?"

I didn't quite manage to close my eyes before the lights in the room came on.

"You're awake?"

I moaned as if I'd just woken up.

"Sit up," she said. She yanked my head up and put two more pillows underneath it, propping me up.

"No more pills for you. You're going back to your own cabin. I'm going to have to enact Plan B."

"What?" My throat was dry, the words came out in a garbled scratchy mess. I hid my relief. Back to my own room. I would live. But what was Plan B? I watched as she grabbed the pill bottle and slipped it into the pocket of her loose linen pants.

"The doctor is going to be here any minute. We need to get you ready. You need to go back to your own cabin."

"Okay," I said. I sat up and threw my legs over the side of the bed. The effort made me feel slightly dizzy. Natasha made no move to help me. I stood and gripping the mattress made my way to the small bathroom. When I was done, Natasha was still standing in the same spot.

She narrowed her eyes at me, and her brow creased. "How do you feel?" she asked in an accusatory tone.

I felt like shit, which is the only reason I wasn't up kicking her ass. I needed to use my brains. I needed to be smart. I needed to prove she was drugging me. I needed to keep her off-guard until I could do something about her. Because right then I remembered what had been on the edge of my consciousness the whole time I was drugged.

Now I just needed more evidence to prove it.

The ding of the elevator sent Natasha toward the door, but it looked like she was reluctant to leave me. I perched on the edge of the bed. There was no way I was getting back under the covers unless it was in my own suite. Something was wrong and I needed space and to clear my head.

After a few seconds, I heard voices in the main room.

"She doesn't seem to be getting better as fast as you'd hoped. And, I'm sorry, I don't think I can be nurse anymore."

"I understand. But I'm concerned. She should be improving by now. Perhaps we should take her ashore to the hospital in Lisbon," Dr. Ashe said as she walked into the room alone.

"Doctor, I think maybe Natasha was giving me the wrong pills. Were they supposed to be blue?"

Dr. Ashe's forehead creased. "No. Hold on." She looked around. "Where are they?"

"I think she took them."

"Natasha?" the doctor called out.

Natasha poked her head in the doorway.

"The pills for Miss Santella? Can you bring me the bottle?"

"Of course," she said and disappeared.

The doctor looked at me uncertainly. I could tell she thought I might be a little confused.

Natasha reappeared and handed the doctor the bottle. Dr. Ashe looked at the label, nodded, then twisted the cap and peered inside. She held the bottle out to me so I could see. Little white pills.

"That's not what she was giving me."

I reached underneath my pillow. There was nothing there.

The doctor's forehead scrunched up. Natasha wouldn't meet my eyes.

"I think once we arrive in Lisbon, you should get checked out at the hospital there," Dr. Ashe said. "Your concussion appears to be worse than I thought, and I'd prefer you get checked out at a state-of-the-art facility."

Natasha, who was standing with her arms crossed over her chest, watched me with narrowed eyes.

Just then the elevator door dinged and Detective Solange stepped out. She glanced uncertainly from me to Natasha to the doctor.

"Would it be possible for me to speak to Mrs. Ainsley alone?" she said. Dr. Ashe said her goodbyes and stepped into the elevator. I didn't budge.

The elevator door slid closed.

I spotted my bag on the couch. I grabbed it and started toward the elevator, but then turned back to Natasha. "Natasha, I'm a little fuzzy still. Can you go over again what happened in Tangier? I'm still trying to make sense of it. Where were you when I was attacked?"

She crossed her arms and, for a brief second, an annoyed look flashed across her face. It was so quick I almost wondered if I had imagined it.

With an exaggerated sigh, she blew out a puff of air that made her thick fringe of red bangs flutter. "I already told you. I was looking in a back bedroom for Sharon Long. I'd followed her down the alley. I was hoping to talk to her. She'd made some comment when I ran into her at the medina. She'd said something like, 'Ask your new friend how Henry died.' And then she took off down the alley."

I froze. Was she fucking kidding? She'd never told me this. I stared at her, waiting for her to look away. Instead, she met my gaze steadily for a few seconds then turned to look at Solange.

"It shouldn't be my job to do your investigating. This is your fault. Gia has a head injury because of you, really, when it comes down to it."

Her defense of me rang hollow.

The detective looked from one of us to the other without saying a word.

"We have a problem," Solange finally said.

"Yes?" Natasha stood erect, tense.

"We can't seem to locate Sharon Long."

"Figures," Natasha said, and turned to pour herself a drink. I watched as, with her back to us, she downed a shot of vodka.

"What do you mean you can't locate her?" I asked.

"We know she went ashore in Tangier, but she never reboarded the ship."

"She killed Henry," Natasha shrieked the words. "Oh, my God. I told you. She fled because she knew we were on to her."

I stared at Natasha. Nothing was adding up. I started to question the events of the past few days. Maybe the painkillers had done a number on me. Something else didn't add up.

"I don't understand," I said. "I thought you were watching who came and went from the port?"

Solange pressed her lips tightly together before answering.

"Our systems indicated that her card had been swiped to reboard the ship, but when we went to her cabin to speak to her, it was empty. It has remained empty."

"Maybe she's having a sleepover somewhere," I said, eyeing Natasha. "And besides, don't you have cameras everywhere. And facial recognition software."

Solange shook her head. "Because of the sensitive nature of our prestigious clients, that is one feature that has been disabled on this particular vessel."

"The cameras or the software?"

She sighed. "For the most part, both. We have limited cameras, but mostly in the pool area and in the stairwells."

"But she swiped her card to reboard?"

"We believe someone else used her card to allow us to think she reboarded."

"Do you think she paid someone to do that?" Natasha said.

Solange shrugged. "Now, I have to ask you to excuse us while I speak further with Mrs. Ainsley."

I punched the elevator button and stepped inside without saying goodbye.

15

THINGS AREN'T ADDING UP

Back in the safety of my own suite, I slept for two days. Whenever I surfaced from crazy nightmares, I'd call room service to deliver orange juice, soups, and smoothies. I'd bring my food back to bed, eat and drink and fall back asleep.

Natasha never called. Never visited. Though I did once dream that she was standing over my bed in the dark. But I woke, heart pounding, to an empty room.

On the third day, woke up refreshed and like my old self again. I dressed and headed for the penthouse. I needed some answers.

The key code didn't work. Then I remembered they'd had to replace the code. I dialed Natasha's line from the phone in the penthouse elevator lobby.

"I need the new code. I'm coming up." I was too weary to say more.

"I don't trust you."

I exhaled. "Whatever. Let me in. We need to talk."

"I think you might have had something to do with Henry's murder."

"That's ridiculous."

"Is it? Then why did Sharon Long tell me to ask you about it?"

"Maybe because she's crazy and wanted to blame me—wanted suspicion on me instead of her? How would I know?"

"I don't know you. We just met a few weeks ago. How do I know your whole plan hasn't been to make friends with me so you could get close to Henry and murder him?"

"I thought you were convinced that Sharon Long killed him?"

"Maybe you are in on it together" I could feel her fury through the phone. "I don't know anything. All I know is he's gone. There was blood. He didn't bash *himself* in the head and then throw himself overboard. Someone did it *to* him."

"Let's talk," I said. "I've got some questions for you. Things aren't adding up here, Natasha."

"Forget it. Don't call me again."

16

GREEK GODDESS

When I got back to my suite, I flung open the door only to find Detective Solange in my cabin with two security guards flanking her. My room had been tossed. The covers on my bed had been stripped and thrown on the floor. All the drawers were open. My hangers swung empty. All my clothes were piled on the bed.

"Room service will restore order here," Solange said. She was sitting erectly in one of the chairs at my café table near the sliding glass door to my balcony. "Please sit."

"I'm busy."

"I'm sure you have a moment." She remained unruffled.

"Actually, I don't." I stood my ground, arms crossed at my chest, glaring at her. "What the hell is going on here?"

"We can do this here. Or at my office, which, I must say," she said, glancing around, "is less accommodating than your suite."

Turning on my heel, I headed toward the bar in the corner of my suite and poured myself three fingers of bourbon. I downed it, lit a cigarette, and plunked on my couch, putting my feet on the coffee table. "Fine," I said, smoke curling from my mouth.

Detective Solange rose, crossed the room, and perched primly on the edge of the couch opposite me, staring. I stared back. Two could play this game.

If she thought I was going to provide evidence to help her nail Natasha, she was wrong. I had my suspicions, sure, but I wasn't saying jack shit until I had a chance to confront Natasha and listen to her explanation. I owed her that.

We sat there in silence. The two guards stood by the door, not moving.

Finally, I raised an eyebrow and blew smoke straight across the couch at her face.

She didn't flinch. In fact, she reached over to the table for my blue pack of Dunhills. Right before scooping it up, she paused and looked over at me.

"May I?"

I shrugged. As far as I was concerned she was an incompetent cartoon detective. "Where did you say you worked before this cushy gig?"

She ignored me. Of course, she did.

"We found something interesting in your cabin."

I shook my head as if to clear it. "Why are you here in the first place? What is going on?"

"Mrs. Ainsley seems to think you might be hiding something. Turns out she was right."

"What?" I scrunched up my face. "I'm not hiding shit. You're barking up the wrong tree. Why else do you think Sharon Long went missing."

The detective exchanged a look with the security guard and then cleared her throat.

"Sharon Long is not actually missing."

"She's not?" I sat up straighter. "Did you arrest her?"

"Her body was found in Tangier. In the house next door to where you were allegedly attacked."

"Allegedly? Have you seen my fucking head wound?" I was furious. And then the words sank in. "Her body? How did she die?"

But I already knew the answer.

"She was murdered."

I closed my eyes for a second and shook my head. When I opened my eyes again, Solange stood.

"That's why we are here."

"I don't understand."

She nodded, and the man against my closet stepped aside. My closet door was open. My clothes were pulled aside. At first I didn't know what they wanted me to see. But then I saw it. A small marble statue of a Greek goddess. But there was something wrong with it. The head was rust colored. I rose from the couch, tilted my head and squinted.

The color wasn't natural. It was dried blood. And something else.

"What the fuck is that?"

"You tell us." Solange's eyes were flat black.

"I've never seen it before."

Solange did not respond.

"I have no idea how it got in my closet."

"It is from Mr. and Mrs. Ainsley's penthouse suite. Mrs. Ainsley reported it missing the night of her husband's disappearance. I'd like to ask where you were on the night Henry Ainsley disappeared?"

That's when I realized that they had never questioned me about Henry's disappearance. In retrospect, failing to interview me seemed like an obvious misstep in the investigation.

"Natasha and I had plans for after dinner, but when she arrived, she looked like she'd been crying and Henry seemed angry. I'd never seen him like that before."

"How long have you known Mr. and Mrs. Ainsley."

"I met them the day we left Barcelona."

She nodded, pressing her lips together. "You did not know them before this trip?"

I shook my head.

She leaned back against the wall and crossed her arms, her gaze never leaving me.

I continued. "They excused themselves early. After dinner, I went to the bar—the Star Bar—the one on the Baja Deck. After that, I got a bottle and went out onto the Sun Deck. I fell asleep on one of the lounge chairs. When I woke, I headed to the Riviera Deck, and that's when I heard Natasha scream. I rushed to the penthouse with two of your security team, and we called you."

"Did anyone see you after you fell asleep on the lounger?"

Making a face, I shook my head. "I don't know. I was asleep. But there wasn't anybody around that I know of. The Sun Deck was deserted at that hour."

Solange nodded, and one of the guards leaned into the closet and, with a gloved hand, picked up the statue and slipped it into a plastic bag.

The detective turned toward the door. "We will have to wait to examine this when we are in port at Lisbon. Right now, my inclination is to keep you aboard until we determine whether this statue has Mr. Ainsley's blood on it. You won't be allowed to disembark. Do you understand?"

Anger flared through me. I stood abruptly as the two guards stepped into the hall, and Solange stood in the doorway with an eyebrow raised.

"I'm not staying on board just because you think it's a good idea. Dr. Ashe told me I should get a proper MRI scan in Lisbon. Now, you're saying I am a prisoner? Am I under arrest? I'm not convinced you are even allowed to detain me."

"Oh, we are." She gave a smug smile and left, the door shutting soundly behind her.

I opened the door and leaned my head out. "One thing, Detective."

She paused, but didn't turn around.

"For fuck's sakes, just listen for a second. If, *just if*, I had used that statue to harm Henry, why would it still be in my closet? If I were a killer..."

I paused as some passengers rushed by to get away from the crazy lady.

"If I were a killer," I repeated, "as you seem to be implying, why wouldn't I get rid of the evidence as soon as I could? Say, throw it overboard? Or, even ditch somewhere in Morocco? It doesn't make any sense that I would keep it in my room. Why don't you chew on that while you're eating your pâté tonight?"

She didn't move.

"You can't hold me."

Finally, she turned. "Actually, I can," she said. "I can hold you in our version of a brig. It's a little cabin with a bed and bathroom. It's actually very nice. Not as nice as this room, though. I'm doing you the courtesy of letting you stay in your suite as long as you agree to cooperate."

I slammed the door and leaned back on it, every nerve jangling with fury.

17

DOCTOR'S ORDERS

I poured another huge slug of bourbon, downed it and changed into my black bikini—the one that left nothing to the imagination.

Time to follow the doctor's orders. Sort of. I was headed to the pool and, sure, I'd sit and relax for a little while, but what I really wanted was to forget about the conversation I'd just had.

To do that I needed a distraction. Some company. Male company. Some mindless rough sex to get my mind off how fucked I was. Because I was royally, phenomenally fucked. In an I-might-go-down-for-murder kind of way.

Deep inside, I knew I was taking the easy way out. Escapism. I'd made it an art form. When my life fell apart, I inevitably turned to drinking, drugs, and sex.

But being considered a murder suspect with the bloody murder weapon found in your room? Yeah, that was a new low. And the suspect in the first murder was dead and they thought I'd offed her, as well. Super-duper fucked.

Fuck it. Booze and sex was in order.

Grabbing my gray Turkish towel and a woven basket filled with more booze, sunscreen, and a book, I left my cabin.

At the pool, I glanced around. Most of the lounge chairs were empty. A few women in their late 60s or 70s with toned bodies and lightly tanned skin sprawled, eyes hidden behind dark sunglasses. I raised a mental glass to them. Money might not buy happiness, but it apparently bought a personal trainer and nutritionist. These women were smoking hot seniors.

But no boys. Not a single one.

After I slicked on coconut-scented suntan oil, I stretched out in my own lounge chair, keeping it propped upright enough for me to take in my surroundings behind my own massive, black sunglasses. The pool remained deserted. Where was everybody? Then I remembered that it was Casino Day. The ship had brought in dealers from Monte Carlo and had a regular casino set up on the Baja Deck where people could play roulette, poker, baccarat, and so on.

No limits, either.

Too rich for my blood. I had plenty of money to spare, but I didn't believe in throwing it away like that.

But that's where the men would be. I glanced down at my bikini. Although it might cause a sensation if I walked into the makeshift casino this way, it would probably also get me tossed on my ass. The invite to Casino Day had said formal attire. Downing the last of the margarita I'd ordered, I gathered my belongings. I'd go change and stalk my man prey at the baccarat table.

When the elevator door opened from the pool deck, two pre-teen boys stood inside with their heads dipped to their phones deep in conversation. They didn't even look up. I pressed the button to my deck and yawned.

The boys were Americans. At first, their conversation droned in an out of one ear, but then I heard a name that sounded familiar.

"Jessica Jones is hot."

I scrunched my face up. Why was that name familiar?

"I heard a rumor she's going to be in *Avengers: Infinity Wars*," the other boy said.

I tuned in. *Jessica Jones*. It was the character that Natasha had said I looked like.

"No way, man. I saw the cast list. They dissed her."

"Too bad. She slays." The boy held his oversized phone up to his friend.

I scooted closer and slanted my eyes toward his screen. The woman wore crappy jeans with holes in the knees. I would never dress like that. But maybe our hair and eyes were a little bit alike. Then the footage changed, and another woman appeared on the screen. She had long red hair.

"Natasha Romanoff is my BAE," the other boy said. "You can have Jessica."

"Hey, I thought her name was Laura?" the other boy said.

"It is. Natasha is her alias, dumb shit."

A cold chill ran across my scalp.

The elevator doors opened. The kids filed out and the doors slithered closed, leaving me to my dark realization. I thought about the stack of passports I found in the silver case. Finally, the door opened on my deck.

In my room, I sat on the edge of my bed and used my phone to search for information on the *Avengers* and "Natasha."

Holy shit. All the passports I found contained names that this Natasha character used as aliases: Laura, Nancy, Yelena, Czarina, Nadine.

I continued reading. Then I froze.

The kicker? The character's code name.

Black Widow.

Sharon Long wasn't the Black Widow. Natasha was. Holy fuck.

Well, that explained a lot.

Natasha hesitating on the last excursion—because she knew Henry would be dead by then. Natasha making the statement, "He didn't bash himself in the head and then throw himself overboard." How had she known that was how he'd died unless she'd done it herself? Of course, she must've planted the statue in my closet that morning we went to Tangier and she stopped by my suite. I'd never for a second thought she'd killed Henry based solely on the fact that she was so petite. It didn't seem possible that she would have the strength to knock Henry out or toss him overboard. But then I hadn't seen her Hopak moves yet either. It wasn't proof, but I knew I was right.

While I felt jubilant, I also felt an inexplicable sadness.

The one female friend I had made was using me. To get away with murder, no less.

I brushed away the hurt feelings. Fuck her. Fuck having friends. Fuck all of it.

My job now was to make sure Natasha paid.

Now to convince Detective Solange.

18

TWO DEAD BODIES ARE PLENTY

When I walked into the small office, detective Solange hung up the phone in her hand.

"I was just dialing your suite."

I raised an eyebrow. Her two security goons stood by the door. I took them in. No gun holsters, just nightsticks.

"I have consulted with the captain and the authorities in Lisbon, and we believe it will be best to have you locked up for the remainder of the voyage. Two dead bodies are plenty."

"You're crazy." I involuntarily backed toward the door, but found myself pressed against the thick chest of one of the security guards.

"Karl will escort you to the brig. But as I said, it is not really a brig or jail. It's just a secure state room. You will be quite comfortable, I'm sure."

"I don't understand."

Solange folded her hands together on her desk.

"Dr. Ashe looked at the substance under a microscope in the lab for me and determined the statue had brain matter on it."

"Natasha killed her husband," I said. "She's a black widow. I'm sure she's left a string of dead husbands behind. Henry is only the latest."

Solange looked at me like I was crazy. I knew without proof it sounded far-fetched and possibly a desperate attempt to deflect attention from me, but I had no choice. I didn't have time to try to prove it. They wanted me locked up asap where I wouldn't be able to prove shit.

"If you look in the case in her closet you'll see that I'm right," I continued.

Solange kept a straight face. "Natasha warned us that you would try to put the blame on her."

"Can she explain the five different passports in her little silver case?"

For a second, Solange's face showed a sliver of uncertainty, but then she gave a nod toward the security guards behind me.

I jabbed my elbow up and back and connected with Karl's thick jaw at the same time, I whirled and knifed the edge of my palm into his throat. In another fluid movement, I withdrew his nightstick and swung it up into the other guard's groin as he moved toward me. He howled and sunk to the ground. The first guard, Karl, had somehow recovered from my neck punch and managed to get in a closed-fisted blow to my face before I was able to take out his kneecaps with the nightstick, sending him to the floor. With both men collapsed and groaning, I turned to face Solange. The whole thing had taken less than five seconds, but it had given her time to arm herself.

She stood behind her desk, face bright red, arms extended, both hands grasping a massive silver handgun pointed my way.

"*Plus un geste! On ne bouge plus! Ne bougez plus!*"

I didn't speak French, but I got the gist. Without looking, I reached behind me and twisted the doorknob, opening the door.

"*Ne bougez plus!*"

I watched her eyes. She wouldn't pull the trigger. I raced out of the office and down the hall. I had nowhere to run.

What was I going to do? Jump overboard?

Fuck me.

I ran. I headed for the door marked "Stairwell" and took off toward the upper decks. For some reason higher felt safer. But as soon as I ducked into the stairwell, I saw a security camera bolted to the corner near the ceiling. I remembered that Solange had said they had some cameras operational.

I was still holding the security guard's nightstick. I got a running start, jumped up, and whacked the camera, hearing the satisfying crunch of plastic and metal. The red light stopped blinking, so I figured it worked. I did the same on the next level and the next. Then I raced back down to the landing with the first broken camera and slipped out into the passageway. Having them search three decks would buy me some time.

In the hall, I searched the ceilings but didn't see any more security cameras.

A group of men turned into the hall at the opposite end. All sandy-haired. Scandinavians, I'd bet. I was still in my bikini.

It was a long hallway, and several men peeled off, unlocking cabin doors and giving me sideways glances before slipping inside. By the time I met up with them, only one man remained.

"I know this sounds crazy. But I need your help. Can you please hide me in your cabin? Just for a few minutes? Please? My boyfriend is chasing me. He did this." I gestured to my cheek where I could feel a bruise forming from the guard's punch. I also knew I had a split lip.

The man looked concerned. "Shouldn't we call security? Or the ship's doctor?" He had a Swedish accent.

"Yes. But first get me out of this hall." I shot a desperate look behind me. It wasn't an act. Any minute, security could come bursting out of the stairwell or elevator.

He snapped out of his daze. "Of course." He slid his keycard.

Within seconds we were inside his suite

I took in the man before me. He had nice smile lines around his eyes. He reached for the phone. "We must call security."

I put my hand on his wrist, stopping him from picking up the phone receiver. "My situation? It's complicated. Can we wait. Can I just rest here for a bit? Maybe we can have a drink and watch TV?"

He raised an eyebrow, his arm still outstretched toward the phone.

"Please." My eyes met his. He hesitated for a second before saying, "Okay," and heading for the bar.

"What can I make you?"

"Bourbon. Straight."

We ended up playing cards. The man, who said his name was Sven, had loaned me some baggy sweatpants and a T-shirt that I'd thrown on over my bikini.

But as I played and laughed along, my brain was furiously trying to figure out how the hell I was going to stay hidden from the detective and her goons until we reached port.

Then my cell phone rang.

19

BLACK WIDOW

"The Engine Room."

It was Natasha.

She said the words and then hung up.

I turned to Sven. "Thanks. Gotta run."

It took me a while to find my way below decks to the engine room. It was eerily deserted—convenient, as I wouldn't have to come up with an excuse as to why I'd wandered into a crew-only area.

The engine room was at the end of a long hallway. I turned the door lever slowly and stepped inside. The room smelled like gas—both gasoline and natural gas. The engine sound was deafening.

The lights were dim and the ceilings low. It took me a minute to make out Natasha standing near the door. As soon as I stepped inside, she slammed the door behind me and then stood in front of it.

She looked older, jaded, wiser. She held a massive dagger in front of her.

It was if we'd never met. The woman before me was completely unrecognizable. Sure, the surface was the same, but everything down to the way she held herself—defiant, angry, hard—was different.

I narrowed my eyes at her. "Were we ever friends?"

She didn't answer. She turned her head slightly, her chin jutting to one side. Her gaze reached somewhere over my shoulder, not meeting my eyes.

"That's what I thought," I said.

"It's not personal." She pointed the dagger my way. My instinct was that I could easily take her out, but I remembered her talking about her martial arts training. I didn't want to underestimate her. I'd wait and watch.

"I never expected the detective would focus on me," she said. "She was supposed to arrest Sharon Long. Nothing was supposed to happen this way. There wasn't supposed to be any blood. Henry was just supposed to fall overboard—a mysterious disappearance. I was never supposed to be a *murder* suspect! I had to do something to take the attention away from myself."

"What about Sharon Long? Did she have anything at all to do with this? Why did you kill her, too?"

Natasha, or whatever her name was, had the good grace to bite her lip and look down.

"Another convenient scapegoat for you?"

"Sharon had to die. She found out about my past."

"You mean the string of dead husbands you've left behind."

It was a guess, but when she looked up, I knew I was right. Her gaze was icy and filled with hate.

"If she hadn't told Henry, she'd still be alive. But she warned him. When we were in Gibraltar, she told him. He didn't believe her at first. I had to move up my plan and that's how everything went wrong."

"You are the Black Widow." I was stalling, trying to figure out how to distract her and then disable her.

"You don't know. You don't know anything about me." She flung out her hand. "You don't know anything about struggle, or poverty, or being a girl in the Ukraine.

"You don't know what it's like to grow up so poor that your father lets the soldiers rape you so he can keep his crops. Where your father puts a bullet through his head because he's forced to do this to his daughter. You don't know me. You don't know my life."

I hesitated. Her life and childhood could not have been more different than mine. That was true. But it was no excuse.

"None of that gives you the right to kill."

"Did you arrange for Sharon to meet you in Tangier?"

"She suspected me. I told her I'd tell her what I knew in the medina. She was foolish. She thought she could take me. Stupid woman."

I tilted my head. "Actually, I think she was the only smart one in this whole ordeal. She was the only one who knew what was going on. You had me and Henry fooled. And frankly, I don't think you've been too smart about this, either. Might as well turn yourself in now. It's over, Natasha."

She glared at me and waved the dagger. "You are wrong."

"Put that away. Let's go. I don't want to hurt you."

When she burst into laughter—that familiar tinkling sound I'd heard as she'd first approached the ship—I paused. There was an unshakable confidence there that I hadn't expected.

She spun and I felt the blade of the knife sink into my arm. Before I could react, she withdrew it and sliced at my leg, going for my femoral artery. When my leg didn't start shooting blood, I knew she'd missed.

I screamed in pain and anger at the same time one of her feet slammed into my chest and sent me plunging to the floor, smacking my back on the grated floor and knocking the wind out of me.

That's when I knew I'd seriously underestimated her.

20

OUT OF TIME

S he came at me again, a blur of red hair and rage. Still fighting for breath, I propelled my feet forward into her stomach. She gasped in surprise and tumbled back into the metal wall with a thud. I scrambled to my feet. The effort sent waves of pain through my leg.

I stood, my good arm in front of me in a defensive position. The other hung useless at my side, dripping blood onto the grated floor.

Natasha pushed herself off the wall and advanced toward me. She stopped about six feet away. Her feet were shoulder-width apart for balance. She grasped the knife with the blade against her forearm. My blood trickled down the edge.

Motherfucker.

"I guess your Hopak training was more than just a finishing school, wasn't it?" I said, stalling. My arm oozed blood. I had to find a way to staunch the flow.

I slipped the tee over my head. I wrapped it tightly around my wounded arm, cinching it with my teeth. I kept my eyes on Natasha, wary of her next attack. I gave my leg a pat. My hand came back wet with blood, but it wasn't bad. It did, however, hurt like a bitch.

"I didn't do the traditional Hopak," Natasha said, panting. "My uncle wanted me to be a warrior—a fighter for our country. I trained in combat Hopak. A lot like your MMA fighting." She cocked her head. "You know what that is?"

"You're not so helpless after all, are you?" I said.

"It is our advantage as women. We will always be dismissed, ignored, underestimated."

She was right. It made me sad that a smart, beautiful, skilled woman like her had to be my enemy instead of my friend. Her eyes were dead cold. Flat like a shark's eyes.

All sympathy for her disappeared.

"You are heartless. You killed a man who adored you. And for what? He would have given you everything you ever wanted, Natasha."

"I want money on my own terms. I don't want to be a kept woman. I want to be the one who keeps the women. I want to live life on my own terms. I want to be so powerful that nobody can ever tell me what to do again," her voice rose in anger.

She slipped her free hand into her pocket and withdrew something small and pink. Metal glinted in the dim light. She ran a finger over the top of it. A small, disposable lighter. Mine. I hadn't even realized it was missing.

The smell of gasoline suddenly seemed overpowering. My eyes roamed the room. In the corner, I saw dark liquid spilling from a pipe with an open valve. At that spot, dark liquid spilled out, dripping down the inside of the ship's wall to the ground where it formed a puddle.

Natasha flicked the lighter. The small orange-red flame reflected in her eyes. She blocked my path to the door. Given my injuries and her training I wasn't sure I could take her out. If I could get her on the ground, however, she was mine.

But she kept her distance.

She knelt to the floor without taking her eyes off of me. In the light of the flickering flame, I saw madness there. She lowered her arm toward the floor. There was a "whooomp" as the gasoline caught, and an inferno engulfed the back of the room. Flames crept up the wall, leaving a trail of black in its wake. She drew her arm back to her, still not taking her eyes off me.

The flames began to travel up the wall. I calculated the distance between us. I needed to take her out and get through the door before we either burned up or the compartment exploded.

Suddenly, torrents of water screamed out of a series of overhead sprinklers. The overhead lights went out and blinking, red emergency lights lit up the room.

"So much for that plan," I said.

But the sound quickly died in my throat as I watched Natasha throw her head back and open her mouth, eagerly embracing the water.

She licked a few drops of water off her lips and smiled. "My plan is going exactly as I wanted."

"How so?" I tried to distract her with the question as I slowly inched toward her, keeping my back on the rounded wall behind me. I winced as my foot brushed up against something on the floor, sending a shooting pain up my leg.

I heard a click above me. I looked up. A cylinder had dropped from the ceiling near the sprinklers. It was suspended in the air.

"What's that?" I shot a look at Natasha.

She just smiled and reached behind her.

I looked again at the cylinder. I remembered Natasha deep in conversation with the captain of the ship one night at dinner about the ship's fire safeguards.

They'd discussed a crystalline substance that sucked all the oxygen out of a room.

Without oxygen, the fire would die.

And so would we. Maybe she was that desperate.

Natasha pulled a mask from a peg. "Ironic that the same material that is about to kill you, will save me, isn't it?" With one hand, she deftly pulled the mask over her head and pressed a button near the jaw. The knife she held between us never wavered.

Her eyes were beady through the plastic mask.

That's when I understood. She was waiting. For me to die.

For a second I wondered if there was anything I could say to get myself out of there, but I couldn't afford to waste what precious air there was on words.

I'd have to fight my way out.

Already, I could feel the lack of oxygen. For a split-second I was overcome with euphoria—an inexplicable hope and happiness in this shit-poor situation. At the same time, I could feel a headache coming on. I felt dizzy and a little confused. I stared at Natasha. Why did she want me dead? I shook my head as if to clear it. I knew these were all signs that my body was deprived of oxygen. Then, it hit hard when I found I couldn't catch my breath.

I tried to clear my fuzzy thinking. I needed to do something while I still had my wits about me. My throat was scratchy and painful, and my chest fought to find oxygen.

I didn't have a plan. At least not anything that would work. But I was out of time.

I rushed her, ignoring the screaming pain shooting from my leg up to my skull.

She jabbed at my side, as I expected she would, so my attack came in a wide circle. I ended up away from the knife and slightly behind her. I kicked at the back of her calves with my good leg, and she stumbled.

As her head dipped while she tried to regain her balance, I yanked the oxygen mask off her head and flung it in the corner. She whirled on me in a flurry—a blur of fists and feet and a silver blade—all heading my way. I used the side of my palm to thwack her wrist and the knife went flying. But her other hand was at the ready, moving toward my head. I tried to feint but the oxygen depletion had made my reflexes slower, and I took a hard fist under my chin, sending me reeling back.

The momentum and my injured leg sent me off balance, and I crashed into a piece of engine equipment. It scraped the shit out of my bare back, but at least it kept me upright. I dodged her next volley of punches, keeping an eye on the oxygen mask to my right. It had landed on a set of pipes.

I braced myself and kicked with my wounded leg, surprising Natasha. Pain exploded up my thigh, but I managed to sweep her legs from under her. I saw her fall in slow motion toward the sharp corner of a piece of engine equipment. I even started to raise my arm to catch her. There was a sickening crack and the pipe rang out with a clang.

Fear shot through me. Even though I'd been fighting for my life, I'd been holding back. I didn't want to kill her. She deserved to die, but a part of me still cared about her. The first real female friend I'd had. But then I remembered she wanted me dead. I meant nothing to her.

Keeping my eyes on her, I reached over and plucked the oxygen mask off the pipe where it dangled and strapped it on. Natasha remained motionless. Her chest heaved as she sucked for air that wasn't there. She needed medical attention. The door was just beyond her. I stepped over her, expecting her to kick me or throw a knife at me, but she didn't move. I wrenched at the door handle and then leaned all my weight on the door to push it open. I was weak, but the oxygen flowing through the mask was helping. I started to feel a little more clear-headed. Natasha groaned. She was alive. In the flickering red light, I could make out a darker spot, a small puddle near the back of her head and dripping down into the grated floor. I stepped into the hallway. On the wall was a big red button. I wasn't sure what it would do, but I knew it would summon help. I punched it and alarms blared.

Within moments, the area was bustling with security, ship workers, and a very perplexed Detective Solange.

21

I CAN'T AFFORD TO HAVE FRIENDS

S itting in a police station in Lisbon, the officer handed me my passport and told me I was free to go. I took it with my good arm. My left arm was thickly bandaged. The doctors had told me that I might need surgery once I got back to the states. My leg had thirteen stitches in it.

When I stepped out, Detective Solange was standing in the hall, her back against the wall. She didn't seem happy that I'd been cleared of two murders, but once I'd told her what had happened with Natasha after I'd escaped her office, she'd gone to investigate Natasha's penthouse suite.

They'd found the case with the passports and on a laptop, her online journal detailing her identities and the lives she'd lived. Later, they'd traced her passports, and each had led to the missing wife of a man who had mysteriously disappeared or died. After they took her into custody for trying to kill me, they'd found blood and brain matter on her wedding ring—some type of splatter from the attack on Henry. The blonde woman, Greta, had caved under questioning and admitted that Natasha had paid her twenty thousand dollars' cash to say Natasha had been in her suite until three the morning of Henry's murder.

And to top it off, they'd found the blue pills Natasha had been giving me hidden in the silver case, as well.

With Doctor Ashe's help, we'd discovered she'd been poisoning me while she'd cared for me. They'd had the pills analyzed and found they were Phenazepam, a benzodiazepine developed in Russia in 1975 to deal with anxiety but that could be deadly combined with depression meds, which was what Natasha was doing. She'd been giving me the benzodiazepine with an anti-depression pill each day. At the hospital, they put me on another medication because the withdrawal from benzodiazepine was apparently just as dangerous as taking it with other meds.

Sharon Long had also done me the favor of texting her daughter her suspicions about Natasha and letting her know she had plans to meet Natasha in the medina that day in Tangier. It was good enough for the authorities to press charges against Natasha for Long's murder, Henry's murder, and my attempted murder.

Natasha was under police guard in the local hospital.

Although there was nothing left to say or do, I went to see her one last time before my flight back to the states.

The police officer sitting outside her door told me Natasha was manacled to the bed so I'd be safe.

When I walked in, Natasha was sitting up, her silky red hair fanned on the pillow behind her. It was if she were staying in a spa, not a hospital. When she saw me, she turned her head toward the window. I caught a glimpse of a white bandage on the back of her head.

"We were never friends." I said it as a statement not a question.

I pulled up a chair beside the bed. I watched her. She wouldn't turn away from the window, but I saw her swallow. And blink.

"I cannot afford to have friends," she said.

"I don't even know what that means." But I did. I knew it with every ounce of my being.

I waited for her to say more. She remained staring out the window, expressionless. Finally, after what seemed like a long while, her eyes closed. I listened to her breathing change. I didn't know if she was asleep or not, but I stood.

There was nothing left for me here.

EPILOGUE

Back in my San Francisco loft, eating spaghetti with Darling and Dante, I decided to never leave California again.

The sun poured through my big loft windows, and I knew life was good.

All I needed was in this room. My good friends. And my dog. Then it struck me—the names of all the people I loved started with D. I burst into laughter.

"What's up?" Dante's brilliant white smile transformed his face from merely good looking to knock-out model territory.

"I just had a realization."

Darling handed me another red plastic cup of wine. "What's that, doll?"

"My first mistake was trying to make friends with someone who didn't have a name that starts with a 'D.'"

Darling guffawed. She laughed so hard, tears dripped down her face. She slapped her knees, bent over.

"Okay. It's funny, but not that funny." I helped her to a cushioned chair. "What?"

"It's that—" she couldn't get the words out. She just kept pointing to my dog.

"What?"

By now all three of us were laugh-crying.

She caught her breath and swiped her tears away. She exhaled. "Okay. Okay. What I was trying to say is that even your damn dog's name starts with a D," she said.

"Weird, right?" I said.

"What's wrong with you?" Dante said.

"Lots," I said. "So much. Where to begin?"

Then Darling grew serious. "You know, there's actually something to this."

I took another gulp of my wine. "To what?"

"They say that names have meaning. We meet certain people with certain names in our lives. Some are evil. Some are good. Obviously, the ones that begin with 'D' are your lucky ones."

Made sense to me. "Then it's decided. If you want to be part of my life, you damn well better have a name that starts with a D." I raised my glass high.

But I noticed Dante was frowning. "I was thinking."

"Uh oh."

"Why did you stop seeing that cop, James?" Dante asked. "It seems like 'J' might be a good letter for you."

It felt like all the air was sucked out of my lungs. No fair. Dirty pool. I stood and headed toward the stairs to my roof. I wasn't going to answer that. James was an old story I didn't want to think about right then.

Dante and Darling followed me up. "He's a good guy, right?" Dante said.

"I like him," Darling chirped from her perch under the grape vines.

"Gia?" Dante was not going to give up. "He's one of the good ones. Hell, he's got his shit together and treats you like a queen."

"That's the problem," I said it in a low voice and headed back inside. "Besides," I mumbled to myself, "I'm done with men."

A week later, all that changed. Dante invited me to a party. Well, he *insisted* I attend—for the business.

"Seriously. These are the movers and shakers in Silicon Valley, Gia," he said. "If you want to do something bigger with Swanson Place, you're going to have to get to know them. They want to talk to you. I've paved the way."

"I don't want to go to a party. I'm over parties."

"There are some pretty powerful, attractive men at these parties," he said, winking.

"I'm becoming celibate."

He'd just taken a big slug of beer and laughed so hard, he choked and had a coughing fit.

I glared at him as he bent over, trying to catch his breath with tears running down his cheeks.

Finally, when he stopped, he looked at me, smiled, and shook his head.

"Oh, Gia."

"It's not funny. I am. No more men."

"How about women?" he said with a raised eyebrow.

"Are you fucking kidding me?" I said. "The last woman I let into my life tried to frame me for murder and kill me. Nope."

"I'll send over a dress that is appropriate for you to wear."

"I'll handle it." I said and turned.

He put his head down. "Please let me."

"Don't worry. I'm not going to wear my leather pants."

"Well, thank God for that, but seriously, let me handle your outfit for the night."

"Fine. God, you're so bossy."

When the package arrived the day of the party, I'd completely forgotten that I'd agreed to wear Dante's outfit choice. But when I lifted the lid of the box, I smiled. It was a stunning, navy velvet gown with an open back. Just my style. It would do.

When the car pulled up in front of my building, a low whistle emerged from the lowered back window. Dante.

"Damn. Am I good or what?" he said.

"It's okay," I said, trying to hide my pleasure as I slipped in the back seat with him.

He wore a sharp, black Armani suit. Thirty minutes later, we pulled up to a large home in Marin Valley with sweeping views of the ocean.

After being escorted inside by a doorman, we were led to the entrance of a large ballroom.

Pausing in the doorway, my gaze swept the room. My dress was perfect. Dante had turned and was talking to the man beside us when I felt someone staring.

I looked across the room.

The crowd blurred in a haze of colors and movement. All I could see was the piercing gaze of the most magnetic man I'd ever seen. From twenty feet away, his look pinned me to the spot.

We stared for what felt like an eternity. It was as if there was nobody else in the room.

His powerful gaze had mesmerized me.

After a few seconds, I realized that Dante had been speaking to me. But I couldn't tear my eyes from the man across the room.

Finally, I said to Dante in a low voice.

"Who is that?"

He was making his way through the crowd, headed my way. Everyone and everything else in the room fell away.

"That's Damien," he said.

I smiled. Of course.

Things just got interesting.

The story continues in *Day of the Dead*, the next Gia Santella Thriller. Head to the next page for a sneak peek or scan the code below to order today!

Scan the code below to stay up to date with Kristi Belcamino's new releases with her newsletter! You'll receive a free copy of *First Vengeance: A Gia Santella Prequel*

Did you enjoy *Black Widow*? Scan the code below to leave a review to let us know your thoughts!

DAY OF THE DEAD CHAPTER 1

Before ...

"Your mama doesn't like me because I'm white."

I said the words around the cigarette dangling from my lips.

James rolled his eyes—at my words and at the cigarette. "I thought you quit." He kicked at a leaf on the sidewalk between us and shook his head.

I used a match to light the cigarette and flicked it into the wide, round driveway of the hotel, knowing this gesture would annoy him even more. I didn't usually litter, but I was pissed off. And besides, I knew the driveway was swept like every hour here, so the fancy-ass guests didn't have to step foot on anything dirty when they got out of their Rolls Royces and Benzes.

My smoking was a sore point with us. James was a fervent anti-smoker, and ever since I'd started seeing him again, I'd been hiding my bad habit. But I was about to blow and needed nicotine to tamp down my emotions before I said something I'd regret.

I snapped my silver cigarette case closed and tucked it into my bag.

"I needed a smoke after being in there." I gestured with the lit cherry of the cigarette toward the windows of the hotel restaurant.

From our vantage point, we could see the ambient lighting of the fancy restaurant and the white table clothes and black silk seat covers.

At one table in the back, sat James's elegant mother and aunt. Both women wore Chanel suits with delicate kitten-heeled pumps and perfectly coiffed hair and makeup.

And then there was me.

I'd dressed up. But my idea of fancy clothes was a little different. I'd worn my Jimmy Choo stilettos—black patent T-straps with the signature red soles—some nice black slacks, and a red silk blouse that I usually wore open down to my sternum. But tonight, to be respectful, I'd buttoned it up, so it only gave a brief glimpse of my collarbone.

Even so, I felt like a freaking streetwalker sitting next to them. It was also how they looked at me—like something the cat dragged in.

After dessert, I'd excused myself while the women "lingered over a coffee" so I could go smoke and feel sorry for myself. The dinner had been awkward. The two women had exchanged pointed looks when I said "Dammit."

If they only knew how hard I'd been trying not to let the F-bomb fly.

Hanging out with his mother and aunt in a chichi hotel restaurant wasn't exactly how I wanted to spend my evening with James. I'd rather eat take-out in bed after we'd gotten busy. Because he looked particularly yummy tonight. He'd worn a navy dress shirt and tight black jeans with Italian shoes. The shirt clung to his toned chest, and I have to admit that a few times during dinner I'd fantasized about ripping the buttons open with my teeth later in the evening. Now my gaze was level with his lips, and maybe it was the bottle of red wine, but I was slightly mesmerized by how they moved when he spoke.

"Are you trying to say meeting my mother and aunt makes you need a cigarette," James said. His jaw was set firm.

Why had he followed me out here anyway? I'd wanted to be alone to pout and feel sorry for myself. Anger flared through me. Why had I even been thinking about sex or a future with James? Why bother?

His mother hated me. I could tell. That wasn't exactly the best recipe for foreplay.

"You heard me," I took another deep drag and exhaled.

He frowned.

"Your mama and auntie don't like me. Why? Because I didn't go to an Ivy League college?"

Like your last girlfriend.

"Because I'm white?"

Not like your last girlfriend.

"Because I smoke? Because we fuck, and we're not married? Or all of the above."

He shrugged. "They like you."

I shook my head, my long dark hair swinging. "Don't start lying to me now."

He exhaled and then surprised the shit out of me by reaching over and taking my Dunhill out of my hand. I stared in astonishment as he took the cigarette, rimmed with my bright red lipstick, and put it between his lips. He inhaled, handed it back to me and then exhaled.

My mouth was open, and for once I was speechless. I was even more shocked that he didn't choke and had blown the smoke out expertly. I narrowed my eyes in suspicion as he spoke. I guess I wasn't the only one who kept secrets in this relationship.

"It's not that they don't like you," he began.

I waited, lifting an eyebrow.

"It's that they don't want to see me get hurt."

I closed my eyes.

That was worse than them not liking me. I couldn't guarantee I wouldn't hurt James. I'd stopped seeing him once before worried about that very thing. I opened my mouth to respond but sat there gaping like a fish out of water.

I had nothing.

His face closed off to me as he turned on one heel and left.

I was about to chase after him when a livery car pulled up and the window rolled down.

"Gia?"

It was Darling. One of my closest friends.

I started toward James' retreating figure, but hesitated. What was she doing here?

"Do you have a second? I hate to bother you on your date, but this is important."

I gave one last glance toward the hotel door before I turned back to Darling.

"Sure, what's up?"

DAY OF THE DEAD CHAPTER 2

I texted James from the back of the car speeding toward the hospital.

That's why I was no good for James. No wonder his mother and aunt disliked me. They saw right through me. I was a nightmare in a relationship.

I quickly dictated my text.

"Please apologize to your mother and aunt. Darling showed up, and we are on our way to the hospital. A girl she knows is in trouble, and they need my help."

I hit send and held my breath. I watched the little dots that showed he was typing.

I quickly dictated. "And I'm sorry."

"What am I supposed to tell my mother?" He wrote back.

"I swear it's an emergency. I'll meet you guys at the theater." I glanced at Darling and then dictated more. "It shouldn't take that long."

I wanted to write that his mother and aunt were surely ecstatic to spend a few hours alone with him, aka—without me, but I restrained myself.

Because Darling had said one thing that made me get in that car and forget about everything else.

"I think the Albino's back."

Kraig King was the national head of the country's largest white supremacist group. He'd taken over our neighborhood once, preying on the homeless. He'd taken the downtrodden, the most down-and-out of all of us, and murdered them, stuffing their bodies in massive vats of acid to dissolve. Until I'd exposed him, and he'd fled. I'd regretted letting him escape alive ever since.

And he was the one who'd marked me.

I fingered the scar that ran from my temple down my cheek. It had grown strangely hot at Darling's words. I thought of Harry Potter and gave a strangled cackling laugh. My scar couldn't possibly *really* be hot. This wasn't a goddamn story in a book.

This wasn't a magical world. This was fucking San Francisco in the twenty-first century, and King was a man who could—and would if I had anything to do with it—die like any other man.

There was nothing make-believe about the pure, inherent evil of King.

And now he was apparently back.

I wasn't surprised that Darling was the first to know of his return.

Darling was the unofficial Empress of the Tenderloin, and as a result, everybody came to her for help. Tonight, she'd received a call from a friend of hers. The woman's daughter had been missing for the past two months. She'd grown angry one day and run away. The girl had become addicted to prescription painkillers and they'd fought over the girl's drug use. She'd been caught stealing a bottle of the medication from her grandmother's medicine cabinet.

The woman had reported it to the police, but, as often happens, as soon as they heard the girl was addicted to opiates, they wrote her off as a runaway instead of hunting for her like a missing person.

Meanwhile, the woman had been sick-to-death with worry. Nobody on the streets had any idea where the girl had gone. Every time the phone rang, the mother expected it to be the police telling her they'd found her daughter overdosed in an alley.

Then, weeks after her daughter had slammed the door and ran out of the house, the woman got a strange phone call. The voice on the line sounded like that of a female teenager. She said the missing girl/daughter was holed up in a house on Tompkins Avenue in Bernal Heights.

The address belonged to a rehab facility—a private house where young people hooked on opiates received treatment.

The mother was overjoyed. Not only was her daughter alive, but she was finally getting help with her addiction.

But when she showed up at the facility and asked to see Layla Boudreau, the receptionist told her they didn't have any patients by that name. And when the mother described her daughter and showed a picture, the receptionist shook her head.

There was nobody there by that name or description.

Baffled, the mother left.

In disbelief, the mother hid in her car and watched the comings and goings of the house for a few days but never saw anything except the receptionist come and go for her shift and twice a day a large black car entered an attached garage. The garage door always closed before the mother could see how many people were in the car.

The mother gave up on finding her daughter and spent her days drinking her grief away. Until tonight.

Tonight, she'd gotten another call.

This caller, who again sounded like a young girl, said her daughter was at the hospital.

The woman raced to the hospital and found her daughter in ICU. In a coma. She'd overdosed. Nobody could say where she had come from or what had happened.

Finally, she found out that an orderly had seen a black car pull up to the ER entrance. Two people had leaped out of the front seat, carrying a body. They'd dropped the girl onto the ground before speeding off.

The orderly, who had been smoking in the shadows, said she saw a man with a shock of white hair sitting in the back seat.

The woman had called Darling who had immediately set off to pick Gia up on her way to the hospital.

"You think it might be him. The Albino?" Darling asked, fixing her lipstick and peering into her compact mirror at her massive kohl-rimmed eyes as they grew closer to the hospital. Her lioness mane of dark curls bobbed as she spoke, along with her ample bosom.

"It sure sounds like King," I said. My stomach was flip-flopping, and it wasn't because of the prime rib and red wine from dinner.

"That's what I thought too," Darling said. "That's why I came straight to you."

"Thanks, Darling. But why would he be back? Would he be that brazen? He must know he's still a wanted man around here."

"Hiding in plain sight works for some," Darling said, pressing her lips together to blot her lipstick.

"You're right," I said. "But what's his game now?"

"Kids. On drugs," Darling said. "More than one."

I leaned forward.

"I have two other mothers who say their girls vanished without a trace the same way. Both hooked on opiates. Both ran away, and there's no word from my contacts on the streets. I'd bet my last dime, King got his hooks into them girls too."

I thought about it. "He doesn't play small time. What's his game? And what's up with that rehab place? It's got to be a front for something. But what?"

My mind was racing with possibilities, each more sinister than the last.

Darling smiled and patted my knee. "That's what you're going to find out."

Are you loving *Day of the Dead*? Scan the code below to order your copy today!

ALSO BY KRISTI BELCAMINO

Enjoying Kristi Belcamino? Scan the code below to see her Amazon Author page!

Gia Santella Crime Thriller Series

Vendetta

Vigilante

Vengeance

Black Widow

Day of the Dead

Border Line

Night Fall

Stone Cold

Cold as Death

Cold Blooded

Dark Shadows

Dark Vengeance

Dark Justice

Deadly Justice

Deadly Lies

Additional books in series:

Taste of Vengeance

Lone Raven

Vigilante Crime Series

Blood & Roses

Blood & Fire

Blood & Bone

Blood & Tears

Queen of Spades Thrillers

Queen of Spades

The One-Eyed Jack

The Suicide King

The Ace of Clubs

The Joker

The Wild Card

High Stakes

Poker Face

Standalone Novels

Coming For You

Sanctuary City

The Girl in the River

Buried Secrets

Dead Wrong (Young Adult Mystery)

ALSO BY WITHOUT WARRANT

More Thriller Series from Without Warrant Authors

Dana Gray Mysteries by C.J. Cross

Girl Left Behind

Girl on the Hill

Girl in the Grave

The Kenzie Gilmore Series by Biba Pearce

Afterburn

Dead Heat

Heatwave

Burnout

Deep Heat

Fever Pitch

Storm Surge (Coming Soon)

Willow Grace FBI Thrillers by Anya Mora

Shadow of Grace

Condition of Grace (Coming Soon)

Gia Santella Crime Thriller Series

by Kristi Belcamino

Vendetta

Vigilante

Vengeance

Black Widow

Day of the Dead

Border Line

Night Fall

Stone Cold

Cold as Death

Cold Blooded

Dark Shadows

Dark Vengeance

Dark Justice

Deadly Justice

Deadly Lies

Vigilante Crime Series by Kristi Belcamino

Blood & Roses

Blood & Fire

Blood & Bone

Blood & Tears

Queen of Spades Thrillers by Kristi Belcamino

Queen of Spades

The One-Eyed Jack

The Suicide King

The Ace of Clubs

The Joker

The Wild Card

High Stakes

Poker Face

AUTHOR'S NOTE

When I was 16, I read Jackie Collins' book, *Lucky*, and it rocked my world. For the first time in my prolific reading life (yes, I was the kid holed up in my room reading as many books as I could as often as I could), I met a character who was not only Italian-American like me, but a strong, powerful, and successful badass woman who didn't take crap from anybody and loved to have sex!

Although I had dreamed of being a writer, it never seemed like a realistic dream and my attempts at writing seemed pitiful. So I studied journalism and became a reporter—it was a way to be a writer and have a steady paycheck.

It was only when I was in my forties that I got the guts to write a book. And it was a few years after that I was brave enough to write the character I really wanted to write—Gia Santella.

She's not Lucky Santangelo, of course. I mean, nobody could be as cool as Lucky is, but I like to think that maybe Gia and Lucky would have been friends.

Gia is my alter ego. The woman who does and says things I never could or would, but whom I admire and would love to be friends with.

If you like her, I'm pretty sure we'd be the best of friends in real life!

x Kristi

ABOUT THE AUTHOR

Kristi Belcamino is a USA Today bestseller, an Agatha, Anthony, Barry & Macavity finalist, and an Italian Mama who bakes a tasty biscotti.

Her books feature strong, kickass, independent women facing unspeakable evil in order to seek justice for those unable to do so themselves.

In her former life, as an award-winning crime reporter at newspapers in California, she flew over Big Sur in an FA-18 jet with the Blue Angels, raced a Dodge Viper at Laguna Seca, attended barbecues at the morgue, and conversed with serial killers.

During her decade covering crime, Belcamino wrote and reported about many high-profile cases including the Laci Peterson murder and Chandra Levy disappearance. She has appeared on *Inside Edition* and local television shows. She now writes fiction and works part-time as a reporter covering the police beat for the St. Paul *Pioneer Press*.

Her work has appeared in such prominent publications as *Salon*, the *Miami Herald*, *San Jose Mercury News,* and *Chicago Tribune*.

facebook.com/kristibelcaminobooks
instagram.com/kristibelcaminobooks
tiktok.com/@kristibelcaminobooks

Made in the USA
Middletown, DE
10 January 2024

47576653R00090